QUAGMIRE LITERARY MAGAZINE
a literary magazine where pigs fly

Quagmire: an awkward, complex, or hazardous situation.

Quagmire acknowledges the traditional land on which we reside is in Treaty Six Territory. We would like to thank the diverse Indigenous Peoples whose ancestors' footsteps have marked this territory for centuries, such as nêhiyaw (Nay-hee-yow) / Cree, Dene (Deh-neyh), Anishinaabe (Ah-nish-in-ah-bay) / Saulteaux (So-toe), Nakota Isga (Na-koh-tah ee-ska) / Nakota Sioux (Na-koh-tah sue), and Niitsitapi (Nit-si-tahp-ee) / Blackfoot peoples. We also acknowledge this as the Métis' (May-tee) homeland and the home of one of the largest communities of Inuit south of the 60th parallel. It is a welcoming place for all peoples who come from around the world to share Edmonton as a home. Together we call upon all of our collective, honoured traditions and spirits to work in building a great city for today and future generations.

Issue #1, April 2023

D1003526

1

Quagmire is a writer-first publisher located in the Canadian prairies. We publish one physical issue annually, but nearly every week on our online platform.

PROUD MEMBER

[clmp]   Canadä

Submissions may be sent via Submittable @
https://quagmiremagazine.submittable.com/submit

Quagmire Magazine
10611 116st #209
T5H 3M1 Edmonton, Alberta, Canada

Visit our website @ Quagmiremagazine.com

Twitter: @quagmireMagazi1
Instagram: @quagmiremagazine
Email: submit@quagmiremagazine.com

Copyright remains with the authors

ISBN: 9798388831903
Imprint: Independently published

MASTHEAD

EDITOR-IN-CHIEF
Ian Canon

POETRY EDITOR
Callum Wilson

FICTION EDITOR
Brandon Fick

PROOFREADER
Heather Wilson

COVER ARTIST
Sarah Balsley

And many thanks to all the people who helped out, commented, contributed, shared, and read our work over our first year.

Contents, No. 1

Short Fiction

1   Monaco by Drew Kiser

16   In The Gods by Kirk Vanderbeek

24   Life 2.0 by DW Ardern

40   O Guillotine! by Nikki Ummel

52   Mark and The Girl On The Ledge by Egill Atlason

56   The Duelist by Chandler Dugal

65   The Fox And The Crow Cross A Shallow Bowl by Aaron Salzman

72   High Noon by Suzanne Johnston

77   It's All Still Here by Owen Schalk

85   Our Own Image by Bree Taylor

Poetry:

101   The Resistance by Tyler French

106   Coverless Manhole by Shawnda Wilson

110   On the Helpless Grass by Atma Frans

112   2 poems by Daniel Damiano

116   2 poems by Charlie Dickinson

120   5 poems by Annette Gagliardi

128   2 poems by S.I. Hassan

133   2 poems by DS Maolalai

137   Car am Car by Aram Martirosyan

139   2 poems by Callie Miller

Contributors
143

Short Fiction

MONACO
by Drew Kiser

Pop the red carpet. Roll out the champagne. Put your flashers on camera mode because I—yes, I, Marcus Gometti, AKA Marcus Comedy, Mr. Nut-Allergy, Mr. Naruto, Mr. thrice-daily meat-beater, the former tone-deaf middle-school tuba player and one-time Northern Virginia *Smash Bros* Tournament honorable mention—I, Marcus Comedy, was accepted to shoot straight out of the D.C. suburbs and plum into the velvety lap of—believe it!—Monaco.

Yes, *that* Monaco. The Monaco where Grace Kelly cashed in on her spectral mid-Atlantic charm for a rock the size of Gibraltar. Where Greco-Roman riches from citrus and oil coat the city in an amber patina. Where red means death and black means millions, where breaths catch between 20 and 21.

Monaco, the lips of the world.

So why did they assent to let an unrepentant yaoi addict like yours truly through the nacre gates of French heaven? Perish the thought of Rainiers or inheritances. God's grace is not so great as to hand me a slice of the Riviera sun just like that! Like everything else good in my life, it happened   to   me   by   accident.   Pure, lightning-bolt-winning-the-powerball accident.

You're sure to have heard about ATEFS, or Americans Teaching English to French Students, the one-year student-teaching program alums cruelly nicknamed Americans Testdrive Eternal Fucking Suffering or Annihilate The Enervating French Stupidheads. ATEFS doesn't pay more than they had to to keep its young teachers alive: enough for noodles and butter six days a week, and on Sunday, butter and noodles. Everyone I talked to who survived the program bemoaned the isolation, the tedious grading, the biting wit of the French students whose image of Americans as obese gun fanatics made their patently enormous French superiority complexes so many kilos bigger. The torment was greater for those ATEFSters stuck knee-deep in manure in some backwater Brittany ville, or forced to dismantle their own belle Gallica in the face of the chainlink landscape of the far Parisian suburbs. Everyone I spoke to, however, took pains to dispel one myth: despite my romantic notions, I would *not* find a dashing Frenchman to sweep me off my feet. No candlelit dinners at the foot of the Eiffel tower, no roses scattered on a thousand-thread-count sheet to spell out the words *je t'aime.* I would not find him because no one did; our demand far outstripped their supply.

But I knew I would be the exception. Granted, my romantic track record was less Romeo and more Friar Laurence. Depending on how you looked at it, I graduated college a virgin either because I upheld impossibly high standards, or because an unfortunate bedwetting rumor haunted me since freshman Halloween. ATEFS was the perfect opportunity to launch me free from my stifling celibacy and straight into a world of romance. It had to happen sometime, right? I slapped together an application, hoping against all odds that some gorgeous Bordelais fashion designer, my future bilingual beau, would feel a shiver run down his spine the moment I clicked submit.

They sent me to Monaco with an apology. "Due to the high cost of living in the Côte d'Azur region of France, we regret to inform you that the teacher's stipend will not be enough to cover all your expenses." I didn't understand that I'd been accepted until I read it a second time. Along with the apology/acceptance, they provided a list of things to watch out for: pickpockets, tainted drugs, human trafficking, sun poisoning, jellyfish, gambling scams, and something they called "general French apathy." All of this plus my father's scowl added to my heady sense of anticipation: the thrill of *leaving*, of abandoning this training-wheel life and popping straight into a sick wheelie. Sure, I was scared, but I left this fear at the TSA check before boarding the plane at Dulles, sitting for eight hours, then finally standing up in Europe.

I spent the first three weeks in line. Lines to open a bank account, get a SIM card, retrieve the keys to my new place, and arrange the hundred other things required not to die in a foreign country. I spent the two subsequent weeks trying to obliterate the shame and emasculation of all that bureaucracy with bargain champagne and a death-wish procession of pastries. I won't bore you with descriptions of the city—Google exists for a reason, you bum—except to say that Monaco was meticulously clean, manicured to a point, a sapphire of a city entirely incompatible with human life. It was silicon to carbon, HDMI to USB, and so much as sitting on one of the immaculate benches made me fight the urge to apologize. And the job? It beat digging ditches but only because lunch was provided. Every day, after failing to assert my authority over 10-year-olds whose futures were already brighter than mine, I'd sit in my tiny apartment in my sole chair and cry until it was time to lie down and cry. I fell asleep listening to people fêting down at the harbor, the way they say a man in a coma can hear his loved ones calling his name.

I wanted to die but summer seemed immortal. October found me trudging my way through the farmer's market every Wednesday and Sunday, more out of a sense of cultural obligation than an interest in overpriced scallops. But if there was one thing about my hellish first months in Monaco that made it all seem worth it, it was this: turning the corner from the fruit stalls and the gruff, hawkeyed *bouqinistes*, you come upon a row of the most dazzling flowers this side of Eden. Mountains of them. Mountains!

3

Roses spilling over like a February 15ᵗʰ dumpster, a gaggle of swan-necked irises nodding in midair, whole nimbuses of hyacinths diffusing their fragrance with radioactive force. It was the closest thing to paradise I had ever seen. The market had become my go-to vision to remind myself of the earthly beauty I'd miss out on if I decided to kill myself.

I passed through the flowers like Persephone before the fall, gazing into the mouths of the jasmine, favorably comparing the petals to gems. I blame the blinding sunlight for what happened next, the bumping into a stranger, a stranger who turned to me with a *"qu'est-ce que tu fous?"* in a Maghrebi accent.   He was short with dark eyebrows, hair shaved so close it looked painted on, the same shade as the stubble that defined a hard jaw. Two shards of anthracite for eyes. His skin was olive and dark freckles peppered his nose. His ears stuck out preciously.

To say I fell in love is not enough. I was shoved down into love so hard the mere force of gravity went home for the day. I was shooting downward, I was rising up. I was unable to hide my blush.

"Bonjour," I said.

"You just bumped into me," he replied.

"No," I said, in shaky French. "I didn't."

He stared at me.

"I'm kidding," I said.

"Okay."

"I did bump into you."

"I know."

He was gorgeous! He was the man of my dreams! I felt myself pulled toward him like a ball-bearing in the face of an industrial electromagnet. I knew I had only one chance to impress him.

"Hot," I said.

"What?"

"Hot," I repeated. "It's hot out here. You're walking this direction? I'm walking this direction too," I said, turning a graceless 180. Then, after a grueling moment of silence, I asked, "What flower's this?"

"Lys," he said. Iris. "Says so on the label."

I felt the blood rush into my face like a *Friday the 13*th Halloween mask. When he laughed at me, though, it wasn't cruel. He was laughing *with* my awkward self, not *at* me. And here I was, on the most beautiful street in the most beautiful city in the most beautiful nation on earth, sharing a joke with the most beautiful guy in creation. He called me an idiot in French and offered me a cigarette. An honest American, I didn't smoke. But what was I gonna say? No? If he had offered me that cigarette and told me to eat it like a French fry, I would have. Sans ketchup.

We chatted. What little he told me of his life as we left the flower market and passed by the port felt like poetry. His name was Azi. He was half Moroccan and half French, and he worked as a caterer at one of the ritzy hotels—namely, the Ritz. I asked a bunch of questions, trailing right behind him, catching his quick turns through the winding roads just a second too late, tripping on cobblestones, stuttering out my responses, confusing my tenses and forgetting all the vocab you need in order to communicate with another human being.

Suddenly we were at the foot of my building. "Oh, I live here," I said.

"Must have a nice view of the ocean," he said, as if he already knew about my air-shaft vantage and wanted to rub it in.

"Yep!" I said. There was no use walking with him any longer. This was the end. I saw our lives disengaging from each other, continuing along two disparate tracks like two lines extending infinitely away from a shared vertex. I would never see him again.

"Do you have WhatsApp?" he asked.

"Yes," I said too quickly. "Well, I have the French version. *Quoi-app.*"

He laughed. He punched his number into my phone.

"Awesome," I said. "We should get lunch or something. Or a drink. Or would you wanna go to the beach? I'm usually available at night. Or some mornings. Actually, I could do the afternoon too if that's what works. My schedule's pretty open." The whole time I spoke he was looking at something on his phone. When I stopped talking, he looked up. "Anyways I guess I'll text you sometime."

"Do," he said. Just that easy.

I floated up the stairs and into my room, finally recognizing the inherent beauty of the heap of dirty laundry, the nobility of my second-hand plastic chair, the cosmic *rightness* of all the precious, precious pieces of loose macaroni I'd spilled last week and kicked into a corner. Everything was where it belonged, I thought, as I leaned against the grey cement wall and sinking slowly to the ground. I led a blessed life.

Next came the hard part: texting him. I wrote out "hey" in English and deleted it immediately. What if my Anglicism came across as uncouth, and he decided never to dignify it with a response? Next I drafted the French equivalent, "Salut, ça va?" but axed that just as fast. Far too forward! I went back to "hey," tried on "hello," considered a straight "ça va," and then realized I should probably introduce myself first. "Hey man it's Marcus," I typed in French. "What's up?"

But I could not bring myself to send it. What if Azi, like so many men before him, would simply read my message and never respond? Why did he give me his number in the first place? He was obviously out of my league. My life was a trash bag full of Dove ice cream wrappers and he was a god on earth. I had never so much as kissed a boy, and he had the loose-palmed grace of someone who'd learned all there is to know at 14. And more than anything, he was *French* and I was *American*, an American who could barely order for himself at restaurants, who bungled every verb in future tense, who couldn't stand the *sight* of strong cheese. Even if my interest in French culture exempted me from being an *ugly* American, I was at best a homely one. Most likely, he could recognize me as a below-average-looking American, and I should be grateful for the distinction.

Some people are motivated by money. Some people are motived by fame. Some people, I've heard, do things because they care for others. But I am confident that I stand with the majority of my fellow homo sapiens when I admit I'm motived by pure, USDA-approved spite. Why else drag your ass to the gym if not to show your ex his mistake? Why bother working for Bain if not to bring it up at your reunion? Why would anyone *13 Reasons Why* themself if not for the posthumous apologies that they think are their due? What finally got me to send the text was not the lifelong chorus of family and friends who assured me I was handsome, but rather the mute profiles of hot guys on Grindr who, never responding to my triplets and quartets of messages, showed me I was not.

I would prove them wrong. I would abandon the old Marcus at the airport like a bottle holding 3.1 ounces of lotion. I hit send and waited for the check mark to turn blue, the sign that he had read it. When it did five minutes later, I felt the old, humdrum Marcus pop open like a shaken can, and the new, ebullient me spurt forth like a jet of Code Red Mountain Dew. Azi and I chatted that evening as I watched TV and made dinner. I swear it was the first time I truly tasted buttered noodles.

Usually my day teaching was 50% bad and 50% awful, the too-cool-for-school students snickering about my accent or pit-stains, the teacher asking me questions about defective verbs in English that even I didn't know. Lunch was scarfed down on the tram out of the city to my second, suburban school, where everything happened just the same as at the first one, except my humiliation was brandished in front of 15 kids instead of 40. But today I swaggered into the classroom, broke out an actual lesson plan, smiled at the teacher and even helped a student with a question after class. I skipped eating on the train since Azi and I were busy texting, sharing our bewilderment at why French people loved *Friends* so much. We made plans for Friday night.

Over mountainous kebabs and bottles of Sprite we talked about where we'd come from and where we still wanted to go. Neither of us saw ourselves in Monaco after our obligations had been satisfied. Beyond that, he said he had no preference where he wound up—USA if he could swing it, or UAE if he could handle the heat. On the pier I told him about my past as a gamer and how one time my stepmom had to take a pair of hedge clippers to my computer cord to get me to go outside. I told him about getting picked last for dodgeball and first for multiplication-table Jeopardy. I told him about my first boyfriend, a boy who I only ever talked to on Club Penguin. "The last message I got was from his mom using his account. 'I'm sorry to say but Chase died in a car accident. His sister is taking over his Club Penguin account, so if you see his avatar around, it's not him. Also, if you could return the 30 Penguin Coins you owe him, that'd be great.'" In return for this heap of extremely personal garbage, Azi told me about getting lost in the catacombs of Paris.

"Jesus *Christ*," I said. "You know that's where they put dead people, right?"

"I'm aware of what a catacomb is. It was exciting. And back then I was really into death."

The way he said it made it sound like death was yoga or baking or ska. "What does a death enthusiast do?" I asked. "Date a skeleton? Buy timeshares in a colombarium?"

"I tried to kill myself. Once when I was 15 and again when I was 17." We looked out over the water, at the brilliant beads of the pleasure boats threaded on the horizon. "Gas," he said. "Locked myself in the garage."

Reader, I implore: what was a love-struck fuck like me supposed to say here?

"I'm sorry," I said. "That sucks."

He nodded and started picking at the label of the Sprite bottle.

"What made you do it?"

He shrugged. "I used to be a lot more stressed about being gay. It can be a lot of stress, you know? It comes from family, from school, from other kids. It's too much."

I nodded. I knew he probably would have given his left nut for a family as supportive as mine, or a friend group as well-versed in these issues, or a high school with a two-page yearbook spread emblazoned "The Fighting Falcons: Out and Proud!" I was featured in the center, cheesing in braces and a My Little Pony long-sleeve t-shirt, oblivious to the fact that this wasn't what every school did.

"I used to do all kinds of crazy shit," he went on. He pulled down the waist of his shorts to show a bunch of raised red lines, thin and criss-crossing like pick-up-sticks. "I had this metal ruler. I'd heat up the edge with my brother's lighter and then…" he made a sizzling sound. He looked at me and laughed. "Does it shock you?"

Shocked? I was bey*ond* shocked. I was about to pass *out*. Gods like him don't feel shame. Perfection doesn't doubt. Wolverine can't kill himself with his own adamantium claws, goddamn it!

"Don't freak out," he said. "I was really depressed back then. Now it's okay. I'm fixed."

"How'd you manage that?" I asked, swallowing a mouthful of gluey spit. "Did you turn yourself off then on again? Or did you have to call Apple support?"

"You're funny," he said. He leaned over to nudge me with his shoulder, a simple, friendly gesture that sent my heart into convulsions.

"That's the *worst* thing you can say to someone," I replied. "Because now I'll be worried about staying funny. And the surest way to stop being funny is to try too hard. It's too much pressure!"

"What would you rather I say?"

"I don't know. 'You're cute'?"

"You *are* cute," he said. He was staring at me. He leaned over.

The kiss started too fast and ended too soon. My lips were too dry, his teeth clacked against mine, and I realized too late I'd forgotten to brush that morning. It was perfect. I wanted another, but he was already up and walking. Woozy from smooching, I followed.

That night, we took the glimmering city street by street. All of a sudden he'd yank me into an alley and kiss me, full on the mouth, with a verve I'd only ever seen in professional hot dog eating contests. The walls of Monaco stay warm in the evening, and he would press me against them, his hands on my hips. When I wound up alone in my room that night, with the sensations still coursing over my skin, it was with the bewildered gratefulness of a tornado survivor finding himself and his house perfectly intact—though, perhaps, on the other side of town.

The next day was a haze. I drank a mug of plain water before I realized I had neglected to run it through the Keurig. My morning students, who never got the best version of me to begin with, had to make do with a spacey, gay rag-doll who kept dropping his marker. I could only think of Azi. If I were a few years younger I would have spent the tram ride home doodling our names together in a heart. But instead I stared out the window at the sprawl of the city, sparing myself the crushing enormity of the big feelings by concentrating on the little things: him setting his hand on the small of my back as we jaywalked, his shocking choice of salt-and-vinegar chips, the *Alien V. Predator* code of his burner phone's keyboard where Arabic letters glowed green.

Absent, disarmed, I bumbled my way through the week, trying to tamp down the realization that I was in love. But then my phone would buzz and it would be him, saying hi or suggesting a place we could eat the next day. And in that minute after his reply I would allow myself to love him again. But as my halting relationship with the language of Rimbaud had proven, just because you feel something doesn't mean you know how to express it. Example: the look on his face when I brought flowers to our third date, Thai and red wine at his place. He stared at the flowers with some alarm, like he was allergic to pollen, or clueless gestures of affection. "The same kind I asked you about when I first bumped into you," I offered.

"They're beautiful," he said finally, and kissed my forehead.

As he struggled to fit them in an empty wine bottle I took stock in his room. Charmingly boyish, the place was a mess of sneakers, candy wrappers, spray deodorant, loose keys, small electric fans, cardboard boxes, and weed paraphernalia. His walls were blank save a map of Paris. There was no overhead light: a lamp in each corner suffused the room with an orangeade glow. Frustrated with the bottle, he stepped onto the balcony and smashed its neck against the railing. Glass tinkled as it hit the pavement below. The flowers fit perfectly in the opening, though an edge did cut an errant stalk in half.

Two hours later we were doing the do. And by "doing the do," I mean "having sex." Reader, don't ever let anyone tell you that fireworks aren't possible, or that your first time can't be special, or that you can't have sex if you've just had two plates of pad thai and a literal liter of wine. Settle for nothing less.

I can't say whether the doubt hit me the next morning or if there wasn't a part of it, somewhere, that was busy second-guessing things even as I was inside him. All I know is that it came. This is how it worked: the closer I got to him the more I found him beautiful. The more I found him beautiful, the surer I felt he could never like someone like me. I tried to play it off as a joke. One day I texted "I need a three-part essay, 12-point Times New Roman, explaining, with data, why you like me." After a few torturous seconds he replied, "MLA or Chicago?" I smiled, put away my phone, then immediately started worrying again. My old doubts had found their way to France, skipping over the Atlantic like it was just a creek.

Texts and replies became hugely important to my newly detective mind. I would calculate how long it took him to reply and compare it with the previous day. Then, as if to fulfil my prophecy, he began acting strange around me. For one full day he did not respond to my texts, and I spent those 20 hours facing my own bleakest fear. I grew anxious. I downloaded Grindr just to see if he was cruising on it. He wasn't, and my own profile got precious little attention—though I was invited to a few "parTies" held by "visiTors" who "apparenTly" lacked the "faculTy" to spell.

Audrey Hepburn returned from her first vacation to Monaco in 1948, and was quoted as saying, "Monte Carlo is the gayest city on earth." Well she must have been on quaaludes or something because that broad was *wrong*. Of course, there *are* queer people around—like the left-handed or congenitally blind, there's nothing to be done about us cropping up in any population—but they come and go in a week, leaving the same soiled towels, hairy soaps, and dirty dishes as anyone. There are no gay bars in Monaco. So when a fellow teaching assistant, a bubbly Delawarean named Sue, invited me out for a drink, I knew I was going to be in for a few hours of hetero.

Boy, was I wrong. Not that the bar, attached to a swanky hotel ("This is where Farrah Fawcett died!") had go-go dancers or Drag. But it did have, sitting at a table with candles, at least two other gays. Azi and a stranger.

To his credit, he did wave as soon as he saw me approaching. The other guy—a taller, delicate-looking wisp with hair dyed lavender grey—glanced at me, then started playing on his phone. Azi, looking sharp in a black button-down, said they were discussing some political happening. I jumped into their conversation, saying something that made them laugh. I told myself not to panic. Maybe things weren't as they seemed. Maybe the other guy was just that: some other guy, who may or may not be gay. In France, the jury's always out.

Azi and I made a date for lunch for Monday and he and his companion left. My friend must have noticed I was dissociating, since she asked, "What's up? Are you dissociating?"

"Something like that," I said, and four hours later found myself standing in my kitchenette in the light of the bare bulb. One slip and everything had fallen out of alignment. The macaroni pieces in the corner revealed my own slovenliness. The cinderblock walls proof positive I deserved cinderblock walls. On the Amazon-box-slash-table, the empty bottle of red—my first in France, drunken alone while watching French *Survivor*—stood as a hallmark of my own isolation. There was no love for me in the world, not on either side of the pond, and the fact that I ever dared to think there might be proved I am not only unlovable, but dumb.

Next thing I knew I was sitting across from him at a café, crushed by a cairn of answers to questions I had to keep repeating. "Who *was* he?" I asked Azi.

"What do you mean?"

I asked outright whether they were fucking.

"Yes, we are fucking."

"*How* could you do this?" I asked. My wonderment was matched by his.

"*How* could I do *what*?"

Eventually we got to the root of it, a miscommunication so huge it was almost—*almost*—funny. "I thought you wanted us to see other people, too," he said.

I just shook my head.

"But I saw you on Grindr!" he shouted.

"I was only on there to make sure you weren't," I replied.

He stared at me. "Why would I believe that?"

Some people can recover from a miscommunication like that. Some people can leave pain behind and walk away without grudges, might even work to fix the damaged relationship. Most people can talk to their colleagues without hyperventilating, too, or cover their own rent after college. Not me. I'm just a man-boy whose most recent attempt to schedule a dentist's appointment left me crying and blasting out anxiety shits for a week. I hugged Azi goodbye and took a long walk around the port, watching the palm trees sway in the ocean breeze while women in beautiful dresses walked arm-in-arm with beautiful, responsible men.

I won't bore you with the story of how I spent the next five months in Monaco since a DMV agent probably could do it with more *joie de vivre*. I ate the cheeses I was supposed to, snapped a selfie with the arc de triomphe, and learned as little as I possibly could about the culture in which I had chosen to live. The period I refer to as A.A.D.—After Azi Dumpedme—was bleak. And it wasn't until I touched back down in America that I started wondering whether he would have stopped seeing other guys if I had asked him to. He never said he wouldn't. Honestly, I just never thought to ask.

After a summer probing the depths of a tub of spreadable cheese, I am happy to say I figured out what's going on. Trawling Facebook late one night, I saw a friend from middle school standing on a ridge overlooking a vista of rice paddies disappearing into a misty vanishing point. A girl who survived a cramped childhood, maladroit and malodorous, now smiled, glistening with sweat and the aura of overseas accomplishment.

That was it! I failed to outrun who I was *because I didn't go far enough*. After all, what is France but the constipated aunt of America? If I planned to really shed my old skin, I needed to look beyond the family tree. A quick Google search, and my future path lit up like unlocking a new character.

I hope you saved some champagne and at least a sample swath of red carpet, because this coming October I am pleased to announce I will be joining English Teachers of New Caledonia. Next time you see me, I will be the coconut-swilling, nut-brown Marcus I've always dreamed of being.

Oceania won't know what hit it.

IN THE GODS
by Kirk Vanderbeek

His only purpose in life was to impose upon no one. This informed his every decision. Over the years he'd discovered it was the little things that counted most, those invisible details that marked the difference between others, who were merely courteous, and himself, completely and utterly unobtrusive. It's what found him, on this particular afternoon, patting his pockets rhythmically (*one, two, three-four-five*) to confirm their contents as he stepped out of his apartment beneath a haze of clouds that threatened rain. He looked to the sky and, with purpose, set out without an umbrella.

This same single-minded resolve helped soothe him of any regret when, three minutes later, he felt the first drops of rain, surprisingly heavy and surprisingly warm, but not surprising for having arrived. The forecast had warned rain was imminent, but he was far more comfortable walking to the theatre in wet shoes and a wet suit than he was forcing anyone to dodge the wide, barbed circumference of his umbrella.

If nothing else, the rain would be a welcome distraction from the pain in his feet. He had long ago settled on wearing a pair of flat and thoroughly unsupportive slippers at home in place of the arch-supporting, but terribly clunky, shoes prescribed by his podiatrist. Slippers and, of course, a patchwork of towels that covered every square inch of his flooring, layered as many as five-deep where he'd identified the most problematic squeaks in the floorboards. He did, after all, have downstairs neighbors to worry about.

He smiled at the fond memory of his neighbors' recent shock to discover that he still lived above them. They'd assumed he'd moved out ages ago, or, as one of them had added with a bashful chuckle, dropped dead.

'No offense, man, we just never hear you up there.'

He'd been coasting on this compliment for weeks, and he was happy to find its potency remained strong. His smile faltered. He patted his pockets in his familiar pattern — left breast; right hip; left hip; rear right; rear left, *one, two, three-four-five*. Then again. His smile slowly returned, confident in something he'd felt during his ritualistic fumblings.

A family of four approached him from the opposite direction. They shuffled, huddled and giggling, beneath one oversized umbrella, taking up no more than half of the sidewalk. He stepped off the curb and into a puddle, deceiving in its depth. Water climbed the fibers of his sock, well past the spider-veined bump of his ankle. The family swept by without a glance in his direction and his smile stretched into an ear-to-ear grin.

He approached the theatre and checked the time, pleased to find himself on schedule. It was exactly one minute until the box office was meant to open, and something in the general ballpark of 55 or 56 seconds — give or take perhaps a second — until he'd arrive. This was a winning trifecta of unobtrusiveness in that it would virtually guarantee him the first spot in line, keeping him from putting involuntary pressure on anyone ahead of him, while still leaving a very small likelihood that someone would be forced to queue up behind him, as well as forestalling his arrival from being so early as to risk making a ticket-taker feel even a fleeting sense of ineptitude at their given task. Had his ticket not been general admission this wouldn't have been a concern, but these were the circumstances with which he had to work. Here again though luck was tipped in his favor, as the center seat of the balcony's back row tended not to be the hottest commodity when people had their pick of the house.

He paused outside the door for three seconds, then stepped out of the rain and into the uncomfortably chilly confines of the lobby. The wet sole of his shoe made a sharp *LOOK AT ME!* squeak on the tiled floor that would likely lose him some sleep tonight. He stopped. He focused on his breathing. Collected his thoughts. And with careful, rolling, heel-to-toe steps he made his way towards the ticket-taker.

There too he was cautious, making sure to establish eye contact but keep it brief, to have his fingers ready to receive his torn ticket with a perfect blend of haste and nonchalance, to express gratitude with grace and swiftness, and walk away.

His every move had the power to ruin worlds, after all. This was no secret.

As he walked away — heel-to-toe, heel-to-toe, heel-to-toe — his pulse spiked and his head swam with an onrush of blood as he realized his gaze may have lingered too long on the bridge of her freckle-flecked nose. A quick glance over his shoulder brought relief, revealing a carefree ticket-taker in his wake, yawning and turning her chin to the ceiling to crack her neck with an ostentatious *POP!*

She hadn't given a moment's thought to their exchange. His day was back on track.

Surely his heartbeat would settle down soon.

He unfolded the worn envelope in his left breast pocket, emptied it of its contents and spread a ten-dollar bill and two singles on the concession counter. He flattened creases in the crisp bills with one quarter, two dimes and four pennies. Calling ahead to find out the prices of his favorite concessions and calculating the sales tax to determine the total cost had been an inspired move. Another successful trifecta: He saved the theatre the small surcharge on a credit transaction; He saved the cashier the trouble of having to make change while an insistent, impatient line of others formed behind him; He saved himself the aching embarrassment of interrupting the performance with either an ill-timed growl of his stomach or the jangling of any loose change in his pockets.

Just yesterday, he'd formed an image in his mind of a quarter slipping from his pocket during a solemn moment in the performance and shattering the silence like the *CRASH* of a garbage can lid, then jingling down the slight decline of the balcony floor, pinging between the shoes and purses of others before finally settling into a cacophonous spin, its sonics rising into tinnitus territory as wobbly revolutions raced towards inevitable… stillness. Silence. It had taken hours for his pulse to settle after that vision. Fingers pressed into the tender meat of his neck, he'd counted as many as 129 heartbeats in the space of a single minute. By the time he'd calmed down and put his preventative plan in motion, it was all he could do to make it to bed before the post-adrenaline drop-off knocked him out for almost three hours.

He received his snacks and slid over to an unused section of countertop. He laid out seven napkins. With precise, practiced movements he unwrapped his candy bar, eased open his bag of chips and gently wrestled with the noisy cellophane that contained his gummy candy of choice. He poured his goodies onto the arrayed napkins, removed three twist-ties from his right rear pocket and wrapped everything up in small, nearly-soundproof bundles. His stomach rumbled in anticipation and its gentle purr coupled perfectly with the grin of satisfaction on his face.

The stairs to the balcony proved taxing after the walk to the theatre, but they beat the impossible pressure of trying to remain unobtrusive during an elevator ride. He hadn't stepped foot inside one in almost four years, ever since he'd spent two sweat-soaked hours wedged in the corner of a crowded mall elevator, unable to exit without asking someone to move out of his way.

He settled his body into the central seat of the uppermost row in the balcony, then he sighed and pulled his damp collar from his neck. He inhaled a deep, hitching breath and exhaled loudly, safe to do so in his current isolation. He coughed. Seated as he was, he could rest easy knowing he would obstruct no one's view and there would be no need to jimmy past his legs to get in or out of the row. His own bathroom necessities were completely under his control. He inhaled. A wheeze. If it came to it, he could keep the contents of his bladder contained for a full day. A horrifying trip to summer camp in his youth had proven that he could delay his bowels from finishing their usual job for as long as a week, if forced to. He exhaled. It wasn't a pleasant act, holding one's bodily functions in for these amounts of time, but necessity was the mother of inhibition. His breathing steadied. His wheeze faded to a whisper.

He untwisted a bundle and began eating his potato chips. He was safe to chew them for now, but he was also ready to switch to a reliable tongue-melting technique at a moment's notice. This particular brand of chip was perfect for live performances, taking only six seconds to dissolve before he could spread the flavor around the rest of his palate and swallow silently.

In the Gods. He had never heard of the play as recently as four days ago, but on two separate occasions he'd overheard Prudence mention it to some of the others at work. No one else had seen it, which seemed to disappoint Prudence. And while it wasn't likely that come tomorrow, the start of a new week, she'd still be asking about it (even less likely that she would ask him, of all people), at least this way, if she did, he'd have a prepared opinion. And hopefully it wouldn't disappoint her. It was the least he could do, really.

By the time the lights in the theatre dimmed to signal the start of the show, there were three dozen others sharing the balcony with him. He felt the presence of each one of them in the momentary darkness with something akin to sonar. As though their very proximity caused faint red blips to glow in his brain. The stage lights faded up to reveal an uncluttered set. He clutched his snack bundles and hoped to be pleasantly surprised by the play.

He wasn't. Midway through the first act he realized that the grin on his face had frozen into a grimace. The play was simply too brazen, too obvious, for his particular sensibilities. He was, however, able to create a pleasant distraction for himself by forming positively charged opinions (*'I admired the aesthetic restraint'*) with which he could engage Prudence, should the occasion arise, without offending either her pride or his integrity.

During intermission he never once considered leaving early. He remained in his seat and finished off the rest of his concessions. He shivered and crumbs spilled from his hands to the floor. An awful chill had set in since he took his seat an hour ago. Must have been some combination of his damp suit and the theatre's appalling overuse of air conditioning. He assured himself, again and again, that by the time the second act drew to a merciful close he'd be able to get down on his hands and knees and clean up every tiny bit of food he'd dropped. He'd feel much better then.

For now, he couldn't stop staring at it. His egregious stain on the theatre.

For now, he'd have to ride out this sweaty chill that had overtaken him.

He couldn't be sure when sweat had entered the equation, but at a certain point it became clear that the pervasive, clammy dampness of his fish-white flesh (and just when exactly had he lost all of his color?) could no longer be blamed on the rain.

The theatre lights dimmed. The general buzz of the others settled into silence, and as the stage lights came up...
he sneezed.

A few people giggled, their laughs sending acoustic darts into the reverberating target of his sneeze's violent echo.

Someone three rows up turned around and looked at him.

A performer in the play appeared to jump, briefly breaking character with a smile that could be seen even from his blurry-eyed position in the theatre's most distant vantage point.

As the play resumed, he could still hear his sneeze bouncing off the walls, the seats, the floor, the stage's scant scenery, the actors, every single head perched up there in the balcony.

The sound of shattered courtesy. An echo of absolute intrusion.

Now was to be a time of desperate measures. He forced his shallow breaths to diminish even further. Inhalations already restrained to avoid the threat of wheezy whistles now became tiny gasps. Mere sips of air through his mouth. His nostrils could not be trusted, betrayed as he'd been by a lowly tickle in his nose. Sweat seeped into his eyes. He closed them. A terrible upswell in his stomach sent a bubble of gas through his esophagus. He swallowed the mouthful of sticky-sweet bile that followed and focused on his breathing.

Somewhere up on stage, miles away, a lackluster narrative unfurled as he politely vomited into the pocket of his suit jacket. It overflowed. A greasy, gummy puddle that his pocket simply couldn't contain dripped down his dress shirt and onto the ragged, red fabric of his seat.

It didn't concern him as much as he would have expected. Some extra cleaning would be required of him at show's end, but at least it was a silent offense. Or anyway he hadn't been able to hear it over the pounding of his own pulse that filled his sweating skull. He tried to count the beats-per-minute but was confused within seconds when he couldn't remember how to pronounce the number that followed nineteen. *Twemby?*

Another upsurge of vomit filled his other suit pocket. Another stain on his seat. Another blemish on the day's record.

He rested his forehead against the seat in front of him, arms hanging loosely at his sides, fingers inches from the floor. A groan almost escaped his throat (how soothing it would have been to let out a deep rumble of relief) before he checked his flagging resolve. He centered every ounce of his waning will on his breathing. Inhaling oxygen by the teaspoonful. Exhaling it instantly.

For the next 40 minutes, he truly was invisible to anyone else, slumped forward as he was. Eyes closed, he watched worlds unfurl on the insides of his eyelids. Bright points of light embedded in purple, undulating webbing, expanding. Strangely inviting, that light. Like looking at the center of some far more perfect place. He focused on it, oblivious to the fact that he was slowly sliding from his seat and spilling his poorly contained sick in staccato splashes.

By the time he registered the fact that he was on the floor he could no longer move. Arms and legs had mutinied, rejecting his former mastery of them. His breath came out in a harsh rasp that escaped his controlling grasp, and he mouthed a silent apology to the people whose day would undoubtedly be ruined by the embarrassing mess he'd made of himself.

The lights went out and the theatre filled with the sound of polite applause.

LIFE 2.0
by DW Ardern

They were putting their brains into robots. This was the latest trend. Cute pint-sized robots. The animatronic surrogates resembled electric kettles on wheels. Their iridescent eyes were especially lifelike and creepy.

"Isn't it marvelous?" Richard tapped the holographic page, rotating the phantom model. Phoebe observed him while pretending to read her newspaper. Her husband was getting worse. Same response, same breakfast revelation, three days in a row. Every morning he'd press the blue button on the console and browse the latest issue of Gentle Living magazine which bloomed to lustrous 3D life in the center of the chrome tabletop. Every morning he'd flip through until he found the colorful advertorial.

"Aren't we marvelous?" Richard browsed through different shades and styles of robot skins. Stainless steel, burnished copper, titanium. Puce, mauve, aquamarine. Khaki pants and argyle sweaters. Bird ties and polka-dot shirts.

Phoebe sipped her tea and spread a goopy layer of margarine on her impeccably crisp and utterly bland buckwheat toast, hoping to ruin its perfection and, in the process, make it somewhat edible. She braved a small bite—something, anything to soak up the radioactive pills in her stomach that raged like atomic wildfire and promised miracles.

She was sick to death of marvels. The virtual Good Day sunrise. The gentle lullaby prodding of their Sweet Dreams alarm clock. The automatic sconce lighting and 24-hour climate-control at a perfect 68.5 degrees. World Broadcast & Weather Report updated round the clock with its talking head ghosts floating on walls in ubiquitous touchscreens. Living out their golden years in an idiot-proof bubble. She couldn't even burn her toast if she wanted too.

Outside in the real world, everything was in an accelerated state of deterioration, which half the people ignored as gleeful amnesiacs while the other half waited in anxious limbo for the next storm, the next pandemic, the next solar flare.

She missed the flowers most of all. Before his spinal problems and her corrupted hands, they used to dig their fingernails deep in the chemical dirt every Sunday and tend to the tulips, irises, and daffodils in the domed community garden of the Auburn Retirement Co-Op. After the serenity drones had swooped by on patrol, Richard would wag his brows with a big goofy grin and they'd steal a handful of flowers, stuffing them under their shirts like teenagers. He would kiss her when they got home, out of breath and laughing, and she would arrange them in a curved-glass vase on the table. When the petals curled, they were just as beautiful in a wilted still life.

Now the flowers in the vase had been replaced by this holographic intruder, an EZR 360° that blasted forth its spectral whirlwind every morning like a magic genie eager to please, ripping a hole to the digital metaverse before she even had a chance to settle into the real world over a cup of tea, bleary eyed from last night's dream.

Richard moved on from his first obsession to the next, scrolling through his personal feed of photos, messages, announcements, slapstick videos and inspiration memes posted by friends and family, miles away, connected by the orbital constellation, satellites of ever-loving grace.

"There was another tidal wave in southern California." Phoebe turned the page of her newspaper. "34 dead, hundreds missing…"

Richard doused his flax-seed and bran cereal in oat milk. "Oh why do you bother with the news? You know it's gonna be awful."

"To stay informed," Phoebe said. Her husband often teased her about her subscription to the International Herald, one of the last broadsheet newspapers still in circulation. She liked the musty smell of newsprint, the roughness of its thin crinkly paper. It was familiar, it was real, a touchstone to the past.

"Look, isn't that sweet? Connor posted an old picture of himself in a cowboy outfit," Richard said.

Phoebe glanced up. "That's little Addison."

"Who?" Richard asked.

Their grandson was three years old now, growing up fast on the other side of the screen. She could count the number of times she'd held the child, his soft squirmy warmth in her arms, the powdery scent of him. Once when he was born, once when they came for Christmas at the condo on Elmhurst Street, once the day her son and daughter-in-law helped put their life into boxes and moved them into the Auburn Retirement Co-Op.

No one came to visit. She couldn't blame them. Why would anyone want to come here? For all its automated cheerfulness, the retirement home was a floral-wallpapered asylum where the old, batty, and infirmed were deposited for slow decay in relative comfort.

"Addison... Addie," Phoebe said as if by repeating the name she could jog his memory. Richard stared at the picture for a long time.

"Of course, Addie," he said. "He looks just like Connor did at his age."

Richard drank his nootropic juice pulp and opened up the Gentle Living catalogue again. He swiped through the holographic pages until he arrived at the phantom model of the pint-sized robot. "Oooh, isn't that marvelous?" he smiled. "Did you see this? People are putting their brains into robots. Aren't *we* marvelous?"

*

Perhaps it was the flu. Perhaps it was the questionable Tuesday fish. Richard suffered an intestinal rupture at quarter to two, followed by a minor stroke from sudden trauma at half-past three in the afternoon. So said the electronic monitor on his wrist. So it was reported to the nurses and emergency medical staff that rushed to his aid. He sat rather unaffected, comfortably drooling toward death in a cushy lounger, watching reruns of Happy Days on their slate-glass television. His face palsied in a permanent smile, his palms sweating, his fingers gripped on the remote control, clicking as if it could reboot his brain.

"I wish I had better news for you, Mrs. Fournier," the doctor said after Richard had been ferried away by the gurney men to the Blankford House. "He's bleeding internally and I fear there's not much we can do at his age."

The Blankford House was the medical center at the Auburn Retirement Co-Op, professionally staffed and outfitted with intensive care units, surgery bays, and all the necessary equipment for delaying death. A bright light waystation en route to heaven. A chief source of diningroom gossip for the residents. Bridget Landris is having heart trouble again, Lewis Kinsley broke his hip, Joanne Higgins sick with leukemia. Gone to the Blankford House. Thoughts and prayers.

Phoebe didn't want any thoughts and prayers. She wanted a quick and silent death in bed with her husband by her side, slipping from a beautiful dream into the waters of oblivion. A peaceful surrender together. And now this,

Richard in a coma with a circus of tubes funneling fluid in and out of his frail body, hooked up to a series of winking monitors. It was difficult to tell where the medical apparatus and machinery ended and where her husband began.

"Now Phoebe, we should talk about end-of-life care. Your husband has requested that he undergo a cranial transplant in hopes of transference into a post-mortem simulacrum. It's a risky procedure, but if it's successful, he should have a 50/50 chance of living a satisfactory life in an animatronic proxy."

"Excuse me? What is the surgery?"

"It's not a surgery. It's an end-of-life procedure. Your husband filed papers with us a couple months ago to authorize…"

The sterile quiet of the hospital corridor was disrupted by the click clack of dress shoes on checkered tiles. A young man in a navy blue suit walked briskly down the hall. He was huffing from the summer heat. He carried what looked like a teakettle under his arm.

"Sorry, I came as soon as I could," he said. "Are you Phoebe, wife of Richard Fournier?" Phoebe wiped away her tears. "And you are?"

"I'm Terry Olsen from Standard International," he shook her hand. "I'm so very happy for you."

*

In the dream, the Fonz was teaching Richard how to tune up a motorcycle. Oil the engine, crank up the RPMs, spark the ignition with one solid kick of the pedal. The motorcycle roared with a thunder so loud it made the roller-skating waitresses at the A&M root beer stand almost lose their balance. That's how you get chicks, the Fonz said. Make yourself a man of mystery, a man of danger. Oh yeah? Richard asked. Yeah, the Fonz said. He popped the collar on his leather jacket and asked for an Allen wrench.

Richard glanced across the parking lot at the girl of his dreams. She was leaning on a sea blue Plymouth, fins gleaming in the midday sun. She was talking with her friends and flirting with a dolphin wearing a polo shirt. Why do girls always go for dolphins? he thought. She was so beautiful. The sparkle of her hazel eyes, her blonde hair tied back in a headscarf. Phoebe. If only he could tell her. If only he had the courage to ask her out.

The Fonz revved the engine again, the ground quaked from its thunder. Fissures snaked through the pavement, faultline cracks in the parking lot, splitting a giant chasm between Richard and his one true love. Parked cars flipped and cratered into the breach. Screams of terror, hamburgers and fries flying out windows into the abyss. Phoebe was unafraid. He reached out for her as the ground became wavy and he fell away.

Then came the jolt, and his eyes latched open with a stutter.

*

The procedure had been going on for three hours. Phoebe couldn't see much through the porthole window into the dark room where the neuro-technician from Standard International and an attendant surgeon were operating on Richard. She only had the torture of her imagination, listening to the buzzing, scraping, sawing that escaped out into the hospital corridor. Although she'd argued fiercely to be with him during the surgery, she was grateful the doctor had refused. And so she waited in the alcove, chewing her cuticles and imploring the night nurses for updates while a terrible reality TV show about medical oddities played on the hanging monitors.

She was devastated, and yet every measured breath delivered some bizarre sense of relief. He was getting worse and she was struggling to care for him, especially on those awful nights when he'd wake with little memory of who he was, where he was, screaming like a lost child. Had she secretly wanted this? And if so, for how long? Then she heard the EKG monitor flat-line with an underwater hum. She rushed past the nurses and pushed through the door into the operating room.

A mechanical sinew of wires and tubes streamed from her husband, prone on the hospital bed under a solitary lamp. The surgeon checked his vitals.

"That was your last chance," he said, pulling off his latex gloves. "I hope you got it right this time."

"Yeah, yeah, stop busting my balls," the technician said. "You know this is the fifth one I've done today, right? I've been up since 6am."

Phoebe rushed to her husband's side. She could see the crude stitchwork from where they'd cut open his skull and sewn it back together. The expression on his face was blank, almost joyful.

"Alright, that should do it." The technician punched out a final sequence on the computer. He looked over at the dead body once called Richard and then at the pint-sized robot in suspenders. A flicker of light stuttered from the ocular lenses in its smooth steel shell.

"Welcome to the future." He grinned at the robot, and then turned aside. "What color do you want his eyes?"

Phoebe didn't register the question. She hardly registered that she was there at all, in a hospital room, witnessing her husband's lifeless body. The technician asked the question again. He was smiling. A wave of panic awakened her nerves, an electricity through her numbed flesh. Why on earth was he smiling? She held onto the cold hand of her husband, wishing never to let go. "His eyes were brown. The most gentle brown eyes."

"Nah, lady. His new eyes," he said. "Green is popular, so is blue. Sometimes people pick purple? Looks kind of weird in my opinion, but hey who am I to judge?"

She stared through her tears at the young man, wanting him to feel her pain, believing for a moment that if she concentrated hard enough, she could transmit her wrath somehow in a bolt of lightning that would send him crumpling to the floor.

"You don't want them brown. Trust me on this one. Makes it very difficult to tell if the robot is on or off, sleeping or on the fritz…"

Phoebe let go of her husband's hand. It fell limp, dangling off the bed, fingers outstretched in the empty space, reaching toward nothing.

*

The voice was tremulous and uneven with a low static crackle from its internal speakers. Tin, hollow and compacted, an attenuated facsimile of his soft deep sonorous voice. It bothered her. Especially when the adorable robot spoke those words.

"I love you, Phoebe."

"You are a goddamn robot. Look what you've done to yourself, Richard."

"Would you rather me dead?"

Phoebe dried the dishes with a towel and stared down at the short cylindrical robot that barely reached her knees.

"That's not fair," she said. "You know that's not fair."
She didn't know whether to laugh or cry, every day waking up to the bright green eyes of this cute idiotic robot that was once her husband, whirring on its wheels into their bedroom with a chipper good morning. To which the talk-show ghosts on the television would respond "Good Morning!" To which the toaster would say "Good Morning." To which Good Day sunrise would say "Good Morning." All these machines of loving grace heralding the new day with automatic salutations. Another day, same as every other, ad infinitum, the happy machines beyond death.

Her hands were shaking. She wanted to smash the china in the kitchen sink. She wanted to break the slate-of-glass television. She wanted to scream so loud and so long that all the screens would shatter, all the circuitry would blow its fuses and burn to molten metal in an electrical hellfire, consuming everything in its blaze.

It was so childlike. Richard had been reduced to a plaything, like the many electronic toys they called conveniences in the house. Perhaps this was a natural progression. He'd been losing his mind. And now his fractured psyche had been transplanted into a robot in suspenders. He'd become what he loved. A marvel of the modern world.

This robot with its blue-grey steel cylinder and roller wheels. Its inquisitive green lenses, flashing in a blind strobe. Its clumsy extendable arms and clamshell metal hands. Most of its functions were cosmetic. Richard couldn't do much on his own, except spin in mindless circles and connect with the appliances and digital gadgetry in the apartment through the weird ant-like antennae on its curved head. Playing games with the dimmer lights, changing the illusionary landscapes out the windows, privately surfing the internet inside its computerized mind, reciting what it learned to Phoebe.

She racked the clean dishes. "It's just difficult, Richard. I miss you. I've missed you for a long time."

He had cheated death. It was a practical matter. His choice was self-preservation, the continuation of life at all costs, even if that meant relinquishing his humanity for a robot shell. They had known these were the sunset years of their lives. So unbelievable how fast they'd ended up here. From rebellious teenagers to sensible parents to senior citizens, holding onto the ever-fading illusion of their youth while death bided its time, a crow waiting at the window. Somehow life had been there, slipping through. She had been blessed with the time they'd spent together. She had been grateful and acceptant of the inevitable.

Now he had been reborn and she felt betrayed. His voice, a vestige of the soul, digitized and modulated through its speaker box, telling her: it's me, love me, hold me, know me. Time... everything takes time. Time takes everything.

"Forgive me?" the voice crackled.

Richard 2.0 wrapped his pincher arms around her ankle.

*

Little Addie was excited by his new plaything grandfather. Connor and his wife Natalie watched their son chase Richard 2.0 under the coffee table and around the couch in a game of hide and seek.

"It's incredible," Natalie said. "He seems, you know, happy, considering..."

"I feel like I have a toddler on my hands again," Phoebe said.

"Does he understand what's happened to him?" Connor asked

There was no simple answer to the question. Phoebe

bore witness every day to the dissolution of his root memory, replaced by the rapid stream of information he absorbed through his sync with the virtual world. On some days, he was Richard 2.0, well-behaved but easily distracted by the intricate spiral of his own memory, recalling moments of his life in great detail with little context to what had happened before or after. On other days, he was Genghis Khan or Mozart or Einstein, depending on where his cybernetic mind had led him, leapfrogging through an endless vortex of information. His identity dependent on last recall.

"Mr. Gorbachev, tear down this wall!" Richard 2.0 shouted at his grandson who was hiding behind a pillow fort.

"Some days are better than others," Phoebe said.

The family attended dinner in the dining hall at their allotted hour, chosen with great frustration from the Assisted Living wall panel with its touchscreen buttons for daily matters – reservations for dining hours, laundry, house cleaning, emergency medical aid. Richard had somehow reprogrammed the buttons to make animal noises.

A meow, cluck, bark, and moo later, Connor and Natalie sat with little Addie on one side of the booth. Phoebe sat with Richard 2.0 on the other side. She advised them against the fish special. Richard's robot shell barely reached the top of the table, only his antenna feelers pecked out. Phoebe was thankful of this. She felt ashamed that she wanted Richard to remain hidden from sight, but she was embarrassed to have him be seen out in the public.

The meal was eaten in relative silence with Connor and Natalie alternately responding to text messages on their smartphones while telling little Addie to stop playing with his mashed potatoes. Richard 2.0 ate nothing, of course, and complained about the service nonetheless, waving his cloth napkin with indignation and saying they had no right to treat the President of the United States this way.

Phoebe drank her tea. Her son and daughter-in-law hardly asked her any questions. They typed and responded with a minor symphony of buzzes and pings, absorbed in conversations elsewhere. She wished she could be elsewhere too. She looked around the teal dining room with its ugly turtle dove and laurel wallpaper. The elderly couples spooning clam chowder to their frowning lips. She didn't feel as old they looked, or as old as she surely looked. How on earth did she end up here? She noted the lonely widows sitting alone with carefully portioned meals in pink plastic trays. And then a wobbly pair of antennae, sprouting out from the booth of Donna Whittaker.

Connor, Natalie, and little Addie left shortly after dinner for the long drive home to Boston. Richard 2.0 chased them out the door, telling them to come back soon and watch out for communists on the road.

There were two video messages on the Assisted Living wall panel. She'd missed her appointment with Dr. Voss again. She picked up the phone and scrolled through the console directory for Donna Whittaker.

*

The brown leather-padded gym was located behind a glass door underground in B-2 of the Auburn Retirement Co-Op. The linoleum floor was painted with bright rainbow stripes, almost cheerful if it weren't for the laboratory halogens overhead. The stylish robots zoomed, spun, and wheeled in circles, wild and free like kids in a roller-skate rink.

"They call it the Playpen," Donna said.

"I didn't realize there were so many," Phoebe said.

"It's an open secret," Donna said. "Not something the Auburn Co-Op advertises, but they are very accommodating to the new residents."

Richard 2.0 and Kevin 2.0, Donna's simulant husband, raced each other around the pen, whirring with manic glee. Their antennae bobbed to the soft ambient soundtrack, the lights of the robots flashed in perfect sync to the pulse of the music. It was dizzying to watch. Phoebe felt sick to her stomach.

"Did you sign up with Richard?" Donna asked.

"No," Phoebe said and then paused, thinking hard on this as a vague memory surfaced like a fish in a stream, imagined or just realized it was hard to tell. Richard had asked her to sign some papers when they'd updated their will to make sure that little Addie was included. She tried to dismiss the thought, but it kept pestering her.

"Did you?" she asked.

"I told him I did," Donna said. "He was so excited about it. It was the only thing that cheered him up when he was going through chemo."

Phoebe watched Richard 2.0 skate by and remembered a conversation they'd had the night after her brother finally succumbed to prostate cancer after a month in the hospital. What would you do if that happened to me? she'd asked. Books, puzzles, crosswords, he'd replied with a smile. I'd be there every day. I'd never leave your side. She turned over in bed and ran her fingers through his hair. Until I was gone, she'd said. Yes, he'd said, and then I'd throw myself off a bridge to join you. Because that would be rude. I'd never leave you behind.

Then it did happen. It didn't matter how many times she told him, he never remembered, asking questions about the pills, the discoloration of her skin, her chronic fatigue. You're losing weight, are you alright? he'd ask in alarm, as if for the first time. You need to eat more than toast, you know?

Richard 2.0 and Kevin 2.0 were playing chicken,

lining up on opposite sides of the pen and sprinting toward each other at full speed. Phoebe felt guilty for her anger. She wondered if Donna felt the same. He was still her husband, wasn't he? No matter how much he'd changed.

"Boys will be boys and, well, robots will be robots," Donna said. "I don't know what I'll do. I'm just trying to get through the day."

Richard 2.0 smashed into the plastic barrier and crashed down on his backside, wheels spinning in the air.

"As always," Phoebe said.

*

The peonies were in bloom. A miracle in the chemical dirt. The roses, lilies, peonies, and tulips in the resident gardens. Under the dome, the flowers never withered or wilted in surrender, sprayed every morning with growth hormones and pesticides, protected by the temperature controlled enclosure. Phoebe could almost breathe easy out there. She could almost pretend the sweet smells and cool air that filled her lungs were from a natural breeze instead of oxygen pumped and filtered through tubes.

She'd stopped answering the phone. Invitations from her few friends to cribbage and gin rummy in the parlor, calls from Donna for robot playdates in the underground gym. There were more of them every day, robot husbands and wives skating down the hall, yapping in dining-room booths, stowed secretly in widowers' handbags. She'd deleted the backlog of video messages from her doctor that had collected over the past three months.

Richard 2.0 was blissfully unaware. He tooled around the stone paths of the gardens, tearing through trimmed hedges. She dug her fingers in the soil, feeling an arithmetic ache, sharp pains that shot from her fingertips down her wrist. She shook loose dirt off the lower stalk of the peonies and gently massaged the root bulb.

Inside the apartment, she filled the curved vase with water and spread out the peonies. She sat at the table and poured herself a cup of tea, studying the flowers. They would die here alone. She was glad for that.

"It's all hard work, baby. This life of ours," Richard 2.0 said, spinning in his steel shell and shimmying on the carpet. Last Sunday had been the 75th anniversary of Elvis's death and Richard had come out from the other side of an internet wormhole as The King reborn. "The studio wants me to fly out to Hawaii tomorrow. Another film, I'll be away for a month or so. I know your heart is broken. But don't worry, baby. I won't be rocking the hula with no one but you."

Phoebe finished her tea. She pinched some leaf silt from the cup and sprinkled it in the vase. She unplugged the electric kettle and cradled it in her arms.

"Who's that, baby? Don't tell me you got another lover." Richard 2.0 pawed at her pant leg with his metal pinchers. "Give me some sugar. Listen to this little ditty I've been working on. I wrote it just for you."

The robot vibrated, crooning "Can't Help Falling in Love," accompanied by tinny ukulele music. The song floated with Phoebe as she drifted out of the kitchen and through the living room. The World Broadcast & Weather Report muted on the touchscreen walls, talking to everyone and no one, everywhere at once.

Richard 2.0 followed her into the bathroom. The dials on the clawfoot bathtub were cranked, steam rising like sea fog. The electric kettle sat on a footstool, humming with a soft glow. Phoebe shed her clothes in a pile and slipped in, a slow submersion of her fragile body in hot water. Lockets of her grey hair floated up, dappled light flared on the water's wavy surface as if reaching out to her. She closed her eyes, the thud of her heartbeat flooding her ears. She welcomed the pounding silence, trying to escape the refrain of her guilty conscience. She was abandoning him. She was breaking her promise. Alone in the darkness with only memory, fragmented, untamable memory, rushing backward against her will to the moment they met. April 6th, 1991. A Sunday. She was reading a book in the grocery store, absently stocking her cart with canned tuna fish and garbanzo beans.

Must be a good book, that's what he said to her. That's what started the conversation that led him to her heart. And now 40 years later, all the memories dashed in strokes on life's messy canvas, layer mudded upon layer, except for the singular image that haunted her—the enduring light of his kind brown eyes, how they held her in captivity, how he never stopped gazing at her like a schoolboy. Wolfish, foolish, in the blush.

She gasped for air and reached out blindly from the tub but couldn't find the kettle. She refused to look. She refused to witness her betrayal in the glossy reflection of its steel shell. She submerged again. Calm, collected, until she heard the low tremolo of the robot voice echo underwater.

"You okay, baby?" His voice, so sweet and tender. It was the same.

She surfaced from the steam, cascade trickling from her wet hair, pearl drops on her bare shoulders. The robot blinked in confusion. She turned toward her husband, her dripping arm outstretched from the tub. Her aching hands beckoned him closer.

"Come to me, Richard," she said. "Give me a kiss."

O GUILLOTINE!
by Nikki Ummel

The knife's edge was cold, so cold, against Marie's neck. It seemed to burrow down her spine, slip around her waist, and take residence in her belly. Her knees rattled the packed dirt floor of her cell. Accustomed to holding a chisel and paintbrush, she groped the ground in an attempt to stabilize her tremors. The guard holding the knife didn't notice or didn't care. Lock by silky lock, Marie's hair littered the floor.

"Do you like the feel of my blade?" The guard leaned down to whisper into her ear. "If this feels nice, just wait until tomorrow. What we have planned for you is bigger than this." He flashed a grin, wiggled his small knife at her.

Marie did see any of this. On her hands and knees, she kept her eyes on the ground, on her hair, on her bulbous knuckles, swollen red knots protruding from fingers long-accustomed to hours spent wrapped around a fine blade, shaping, creating. She never knew this aspect of knives, or of her hands; the ugliness, the callousness, of both. She never knew how much trouble they could cause, the knives and the hands.

"That's a good girl. We're almost done. Can't have your hair getting stuck in the guillotine, now can we? Takes too long to clean." The guard laughed, low and earthy, as if he, too, were part of this cell. The living embodiment of the home of the condemned. A man made of dirt and spilled blood, birthed below Paris.

"See you in the morning, Madame," he hissed, followed by a mouthful of phlegm, aimed at the middle of Marie's chest.

Her dress, delicately patterned with orange blossoms and fringed with lace, was caked in layers of dirt, sweat, and blood. And now, spit. Marie looked up at the guard, met his eyes for the first time: they were cold, wet, and blue like the Seine. Like God had too much water on His paintbrush when He mixed this man into existence. Marie wondered what it would be like to sculpt him, to wield her thin blade at his throat, to shape the wax into a semblance of man.

The guard closed her cell door without bothering to lock it. After the first day, no guard had. So pathetic they thought her, so hopeless. An animal too afraid to leave its own cage.

Marie gathered her locks from the ground, delicately brushed her hair with her fingertips. *How long will it take to grow again?* She did not bother to answer her own question. Hair does not grow when you are dead.

As a child, Marie's uncle, Dr. Philippe Curtius, would pluck flowers, place them in her hair, and paint portraits of her in the living room. Her mother, readying supper or dinner, would pause in the doorway to watch. Marie would giggle, pat the flowers in her hair as Philippe scolded her for moving. Paris seemed so much simpler back then. But of course, that was not true: she was just younger, shielded from adult worries and murmurs of revolution.

Marie crossed her small cell and placed her hair in the corner. *For safekeeping*, she thought, and burst into laughter. It ripped a hole through the prison's silence. Laughter gave way to gurgling, as Marie, surprised by her own outburst, choked on it.

Marie's appearance had always been well constructed but since her arrest, she'd forgotten how to wear her own face. The hours spent sculpting others' faces helped her understand her own, and, in their absence, she'd forgotten how to raise a brow, pout a lip, smile. In this moment, choked by her own laughter, her face hung, loose, torn between humor, surprise, and terror. Like so many of the death masks she sculpted from faces after they lay with the guillotine. Like her death mask, after tomorrow.

Marie lifted her fingers to her shaved head, felt the knobs of her skull. Valleys and peaks hidden, all these years, under her hairline. An undiscovered civilization of bumps and patches. As her hands searched this new part of her body, Marie wondered if Philippe was still alive. If he would be the one to fashion her death mask out of wax. He was so good at it.

How did it come to this? Ah, yes: that fateful day Marie accompanied Philippe to Versailles for one of his exhibitions. Her uncle, always the doting teacher, brought Marie's sculpture of Voltaire along, showcasing it with his own art. When asked by King Louis XVI about the Voltaire sculpture, Philippe, bubbling with pride, gushed about his niece's talent. Her cheeks burned red that day— at 20 years old, she was not used to idolization by men. Not for her art, anyway. The King invited them back a few months later, and then again. Soon after, Marie received a request to tutor Princess Élisabeth in the art of wax modeling. She had no reason to refuse.

Marie sat down next to her pile of hair and stroked it absentmindedly. She sighed deep, felt her breath catch in the back of her throat, threatening to provoke another coughing fit. The air in the basement prison was stale, an invisible tapestry that hung over the cells, smothering the prisoners. Prisoner. Besides the guard, Marie had not seen another person in days.

Not that she was aware of time. In the dank underground prison, time was nonexistent. An endless expanse, only marked by the growing pile of feces in the corner, the occasional chunk of bread, moldy cheese, and water cup. Marie tried to keep time in her head, to sleep only at night, but after the first few days, she barely woke to urinate. When she dreamed, she remembered Versailles: the scent of oranges on the summer breeze, dawn's golden light over the great lawn, oven-warm cream puff pastries. These dreams ended the same: the flutter of eyes, a sharp inhalation, a groan, a sob, and the dull ache of loss.

This day was no different. Eyes closed, Marie leaned her head against the smooth stone wall. It was cold, *like the water in her bowl. She rinsed her paintbrush then submerged it in green paint. Madame Élisabeth laughed, the slightest tinkle of bells, like heaven opened up, just for a second, and let an angel through. Élisabeth looked Marie in the face, raised her paintbrush, and dabbed her with blue paint on the nose. Now it was her turn to laugh, to chase Élisabeth around the sitting room with her paintbrush, dripping green. Élisabeth turned and caught Marie in her arms, into a hug, and—*

"You sure do sleep like the dead. Hope you're not, though, or else we're going to have some disappointed spectators tomorrow. Guillotine just isn't quite the same when the body's already limp. Doesn't have the same crunch." The guard's laugh was a full-throated thing. He threw his head back, opened his mouth wide, inviting Marie to tip herself in, journey down his gullet, and find what lived in the cavern of his chest.

The guard jangled his keys in Marie's ear until her eyes snapped open, wild with confusion. Startled, she flung herself backwards, away from the guard. A sickening crack echoed around the prison's walls as Marie's head collided hard with the stone behind her. She twitched once and slumped to the side.

Marie laid the brushes on her easel's edge to dry, stealing a glance at Élisabeth's blank canvas. Élisabeth refused to participate, choosing instead to read the Bible and sip champagne. It'd been two days of this, and Marie was scared. What if King Louis found out? Would she be fired? What would Philippe say?

"You were hired to teach me modeling, were you not?" Élisabeth oozed from over her champagne glass. "Marie, answer me. What were you hired to do?"

"Your brother hired me to teach you modeling, as you said, Madame. But you cannot learn the art of wax until you know the basics of art itself," Marie responded, evenly.

"Ah, yes, I love this part. The part where you tell me, Princess Élisabeth of France, that I don't know how to paint or draw well enough to learn your precious art of wax modeling. Did God somehow make a mistake when He chose my family to represent His Kingdom?" Élisabeth's voice, sultry smooth, as if dipped in the finest of Versailles' honey, did not fool Marie. Marie feared what lay beneath the silk of Élisabeth's demeanor.

"Madame, I am the best wax sculptor in France. I trust that God has bestowed us both with talents. I intend to share mine with you, so that you may use modeling to honor God."

Élisabeth, satisfied with Marie's piety, smiled broadly, a toothy smile that seemed to consume her whole face. She looked radiant.

"To God be all glory, Marie. I will see you in a few days, then," Élisabeth replied with a tilt of her head.

Relief flooded Marie's limbs as heat rose to her cheeks. She felt light, suddenly. Weightless. Marie looked at Élisabeth, risked a shy smile in return—

"Whoa, easy now. Don't move too fast."

Marie's head felt heavy, like she was buried beneath a thousand quilts. She could feel someone's hands under her armpits, lifting her to a sitting position. *Élisabeth?* Reality flooded Marie's mind with every jolt of pain. The guard! She willed her eyes open.

"Aaaaghhh!" Marie's agony reverberated from stone to stone, landed in her chest. She doubled over and heaved bile.

"It's okay, Marie. You're going to be okay."

Marie knew this voice. She gaped at the man next to her.

"Uncle Philippe?"

"Hey, my dove. I am so sorry. I went from prison to prison, cell to cell… I couldn't find you. But I'm here now. I convinced the guard to rouse you so I could prove you weren't a royalist. I'm here now." Philippe's words burst forth, halted occasionally by heaving sobs. His big, brown eyes leaked a stream of tears.

Marie looked at him and remembered, finally, how to smile. "I'm so happy you are here, Uncle Philippe. Thank you for saving me."

"Not so fast, now. You're not free until I say so." Outside of Marie's cell, the guard slinked forward, a smile dancing on his lips.

"I've shown you her art, her wax figures. We had a deal." Philippe attempted to swell, to fill up the space between the guard and Marie, but, inside the prison cell, he seemed to shrink instead.

"Yeah, I'm thinking that's not enough, old man," the guard teased. He stepped closer to the cell door.

"I will tell Collot d'Herbois about this. He supports me and my family. I am here because of him. I will tell him of your insolence, I will."

It worked. The guard no longer smiled. He took two steps back and gestured at the door. "Be my guest, Madame. Monsieur."

Marie, supported by Philippe, hobbled, achingly, toward the prison stairs, attempting to remember. How long had it been since she walked more than the length of her cell? According to the protest in her bones, it had been years.

At the top of the stairs, Marie turned to look down at her cell: the dirt floor, hard and cold. The corner where she made waste. The bars, just wide enough for rats to come and go, rats that bit at her fingertips, her nose. She learned to sleep sitting up. Marie's hair still lay in a pile in the corner, and for a second, she felt regret, leaving it behind.

"Uncle Philippe, what deal did you make with the Jacobins? How did you free me?"

Between bouts of fever, this question had burned in Marie's mind for days. Finally, after a week of bed rest, cold compresses, and sweat-soaked quilts, Marie's fever broke. She immediately called for her uncle.

Philippe, known for his honesty, shifted uncomfortably from foot to foot. "My sweet Marie, you are still not better. Your humors are out of proportion. It is best for this conversation to wait."

Philippe's eyes stay trained on the window above Marie's bed.

Marie willed his eyes to meet hers. She had never known her uncle to avoid the truth. Even as a child, when Marie would call him "Papa," he would correct her, tell her she had a father, and he was dead. She would sit on Philippe's lap and listen to him explain, over and over, how her father died in the Seven Years' War. Marie didn't care what he said, but just that he said it; Philippe was the only father she'd ever known.

Marie cleared her throat.

"Uncle, you are a great man. You gave me my art, my first love. I owe you so much. But I also believe that you owe me the truth."

Instead of raising his eyes to Marie's face, Philippe raised his hands to his, burying his face in his broad palms. "If it weren't for wax modeling, my dove, you would have never ended up at Versailles. You never would have become a tutor to Princess Élisabeth. You never would have become a target of the revolution. It is all my fault!" Philippe's chest heaved, heavy with regret.

Now it was Marie's turn to bury her face, to hide her tears that fell and soaked her bed anew. "Uncle, the nine years I spent with Élisabeth are the happiest years of my life. Do not cry for bringing me joy. Cry that it is gone so soon."

Philippe looked at Marie then. Knowledge crept up his spine. He knew the loss Marie spoke of. It was the reason he never married. It was why he made a family with Marie's mother, a widow with a newborn on her back. It was why he never married Marie's mother, despite their amiable companionship, and continued to pay her to be his housekeeper. There are some losses that cannot be recovered, some secrets best kept for the grave.

Philippe buried his new knowledge of Marie, for her safety, as well as for his. The royalists arrested her for tutoring Élisabeth. If they knew the full extent of Marie's love for the princess, of the depth of their relationship, there was no amount of bargaining that could save her.

Philippe took a deep breath to steady his voice.

"Oh, my dear Marie, my dove. I did what I had to do to get you out. I hope you can forgive me. I wanted nothing more than for you to be free. The deal that I made with the Jacobins requires you to practice your art for them. You will work for them, now, until the revolution is over. Do you understand? You are theirs for the time being. It was the only way."

Marie stared at Philippe. In her lap, her hands clasped and re-clasped themselves, over and over, sensing their lost freedom.

"When do I begin, uncle?" Marie whispered.

"Tomorrow. Marie Antoinette's trial was today. It did not go well for the Queen. They need you to begin tomorrow."

Marie felt herself sink into the bed, deeper and deeper, as if wax filled her veins, as if she were a model to be set up in one of Philippe's shows. The terms of her freedom doused her thoughts like a bucket of waste thrown from a second story window. Philippe bargained with the Jacobins with what he had: Marie's art.

Her mind ricocheted thoughts she dared not speak. This is not freedom. This is a different kind of imprisonment. Cell bars were exchanged for chisels. Her hands, once the prize of Versailles, would make death masks for the Queen and her consorts.

Marie's first delivery would arrive in the morning.

The July sun cast sharp shadows on the dirt road as Marie hurried toward Élisabeth's. The late afternoon breeze twisted Marie's hair around her neck and carried a sweet smell of oranges. Inhaling deeply, the knot in her stomach unfurled. Every step towards Montreuil was a step closer to Élisabeth. She could not help but smile.

Marie's return to consciousness was gradual, unwilling. The sun peeked through the tapestries in her room, a deep shade of gold. It was late morning. Marie squeezed her eyes shut, begging sleep to return. She did not want to live beholden to the Jacobins and their Reign of Terror. Beginning to simmer in her gut was an unfamiliar feeling: resentment. She rolled over in bed as a sharp knock came from the front door.

"Uncle Philippe?" Marie inquired, sitting up begrudgingly.

The knock sounded again.

Marie sighed and began dressing, covered her shaven head with a kerchief and pulled boots over her stockings. It was strange, being back home after nine years at Versailles.

Marie's clothes here, while far more comfortable and practical, lacked the beauty and elegance to which she'd grown accustomed. At least she could get dressed on her own, and with haste.

The knock, more urgent this time, resounded across the silent house.

Marie tied an apron around her skirt just as she opened the door, a tad too forcefully. A young boy stood resolute, a covered basket in his hands. He beamed an earth-stopping grin from ear to ear. Marie couldn't stop herself from returning the smile.

"Oh hello, young man! To what do I owe the pleasure?" She bent down so their eyes were level.

"A delivery for Marie Grosholtz, Madame," the boy said with excitement. He bounced from toe to toe, almost dancing.

"That is me, dear friend. Gladly accepted, thank you," Marie replied between giggles. She reached out and grabbed the basket from the child, who continued to smile gleefully. She could not remember why she was so hesitant to get out of bed. Surely a sweet-faced child was a sign of good omen, especially this early in the morning.

Marie quietly shut the front door, walked the narrow passageway to the kitchen, and placed the basket on the counter. Curious, she pulled up the cloth that covered it and screamed.

Nestled beneath lace was Marie Antoinette's head.

Marie got to work. Desperate to avoid the former Queen's fate, Marie prepared a death mask. As she heated the wax, a knock at the door disrupted her. The boy, still joyous, delivered another head. And he returned again. And again. By the time the sun cast long shadows over Paris, 23 heads and 23 baskets covered every surface of the sitting room. Marie was drenched in sweat from the constant melting, molding, and setting of wax. The room swelled with the smell of blood.

Relief coursed through her as the last mask, a male royal whose name she could not recall, set out to dry.

Marie sank into a chair at the table, laid her head down. Her forearms, temporary pillows. Where were Philippe and her mother? It was unlike them to be gone so long without sending word. Then again, Marie herself had been gone for almost a decade. Maybe she was the stranger now, breaking custom. Maybe they were acting according to their own norms, ones she did not know yet.

It had been a long, grueling day. After so many years in Versailles, Marie was unaccustomed to hard work. This was Élisabeth's doing, mostly. She refused to allow Marie to work with any of the other nobles, keeping Marie all to herself. Marie missed Élisabeth more than she had ever missed anything. It was the littlest things that brought her back: the delivery boy's big smile that consumed his whole face; the white lace cloth that covered the guillotine victims, so similar to Élisabeth's favorite dress; the smell of melting wax. Marie could not escape Élisabeth, it seemed. Her mind overflowed with her.

A knock came from the front door. "What is it now?" Marie cried, exasperated. She rose swiftly and crossed the room in two broad steps. With percolating frustration, she swung open the door and let it slam against the wall behind.

"A delivery for Marie Gros—"

Marie snatched the basket from the child's hands without saying a word. She threw the door shut as tears of frustration dripped down her cheeks. Would it ever stop? How many people had to die in order for the revolution to be deemed a success? When would her debt be fulfilled?

Marie placed the basket on the table where she had been resting, just moments before. She pulled the cloth back and gasped.

"No! I can't. I won't. No!" Marie moaned, wrapping her arms around her middle.

In the basket lay the head of her beloved Princess Élisabeth, with a scrawled note pinned to her lip that read: "Liberté, Egalité, Fraternité."

MARK AND THE GIRL ON THE LEDGE
by Egill Atlason

Mark was a balding 34-year-old man. His mother never loved him, and he was still quite broken up about it. An untucked corner of his shirt fluttered in the wind as he stood on the ledge of a bridge from which he intended to jump and kill himself. Much like everything else in his life, he was procrastinating.

He wet his index finger and held it in the air. "Southwest wind at about ten miles per hour. Upwards of sixty degrees. Chance of showers."

The bridge had been abandoned between two patches of overgrown forest whose vines crept along the sides of the abutment. The safety railing was a metal bar that could be just as easily climbed over and ducked under to find oneself in the shallow streak of river below. Mark half hoped the bridge would crumble in a moment, sparing him the jump. A single drop of rain fell on the pro side of a crumpled-up list of pros and cons he held in his hand.

Pros:
Easier in the long run.
Less on to-do list.
No more thoughts.
Cons:
Need for decisiveness.

He hadn't strictly found an actual con to put on the list, but he wanted to put something on that side. Besides, every argument in his head had been circling toward suicide for a while now, and logically, it seemed a lot easier to oblige. The problem lay in actually doing it.

He thought he was pathetic, a thought that had been with him long enough for him to forget where it first came from. Preoccupied as he was, he heard a timid pitter-patter of feet behind him and turned around to see a teenage girl.

"I didn't think there would be anyone else here," she said in a feeble voice.

Every article of clothing she wore was too big for her, so you couldn't see her hands, or that she was emaciated. But you could tell she wasn't energetic by how she could barely carry the brown satchel she wore over her shoulder. Mark thought she was pretty, which made him ashamed because she was kind of young. Not that he would do anything about it, he was just saying to himself that she was pretty. That didn't make him a bad person.

Mark realized he hadn't said anything in a while and blurted out, "Hi."

She straightened her back. "I came here to kill myself, but now that you're here, I feel sort of awkward about it."

"Oh… I don't mind if you want to go ahead."

She dropped her satchel. "That's kind of a weird thing to say to someone who just told you she's gonna kill herself."

"What are you supposed to say?"

"Maybe something about how life is worth living."

"Oh." Mark hadn't thought about that.

She ducked under the safety railing and got on the ledge next to him. "Do you think it'll do the trick?"

Mark held on to the railing and leaned down to see a drop that may or may not have killed them. Depending on where they dropped, the fall would have had upwards of a sixty percent chance of success.

"I think so," he said.

She turned to him. "What are you here for?"

Mark thought it over. He had no idea what he was doing anywhere at any time. As he looked at this girl, he wished that life was shorter. Not just because he wanted to be dead but because that way, he might remember what he was so upset about—because he was certainly upset—it had just got so muddled up in time. Everything upsetting was long gone from his life. His mother had been dead for three years. He couldn't remember the name of the kid who bullied him relentlessly in middle school. But this girl might have had something upsetting happening to her on a daily basis. She might have wounds so fresh that she could reach in and extract the shrapnel.

"I don't know," he said.

She did a poor impression of Doctor Phil. "That's no good. You don't have any direction in life."

Mark chuckled. "Is that so?"

"Sure is. You just have to ask yourself –" she thrust her index finger defiantly into the air – "what's the one thing you really want to do?"

Mark sighed, and for a rare change of pace, he actually told the truth. "I want to be a weatherman."

She looked almost disgusted. "Isn't that really easy?"

Mark burst into uncontrollable laughter. He had expected to defend himself for daring to be anything at all. "Honestly, I don't even know. Never applied."

"See, that's your problem."

Mark wiped a single tear from his cheek. "Well, what do you want to be?"

"Ugh, why does everyone need to have a thing? Can't you just be allowed to exist without having to be something?"

"You're the one who—" Mark felt himself getting frustrated, so he took a deep breath before answering. "I suppose you're right."

"What do you do if you're not a weatherman?"

"I temp at accounting firms. It sucks."

"Is that why you're suicidal?"

Mark wasn't surprised that she knew he was suicidal, even though he hadn't strictly told her. He imagined that everyone could tell everything about him just by looking. "I don't know."

"What's your favorite thing about being suicidal?"

"I'm sorry?"

"My guidance counselor told me that I could use a more optimistic view of the world. So, what's your favorite thing about being suicidal?"

"I don't know. I hadn't thought about it that way."

"Well, that's the thing, see I turned it over in my head and came to the conclusion that maybe it's a privilege in itself to feel tremendous pain. Not in a masochistic way or anything, but that maybe the pain is something that connects us all in a deeper way than even happiness could. At least that's the only thing I could think of that's positive."

"Then why do you want to kill yourself?"

"I just can't take it anymore."

A drop of rain fell on her shoulder, followed by another. She pulled her bony hand out of her sleeve and held it out as the rain came pouring down. They made eye contact for a moment until Mark looked away. They were both soaked when the rain stopped a minute later.

The girl leapt over the safety railing. "I'm going home."

"Just like that?"

"Yeah." She picked up her satchel. "Look, my satchel is all wet. Besides, you can't kill yourself on a rainy day."

Mark stood still on the ledge as she walked down the road. He remembered that he had predicted the showers and felt the slightest bit of pride. He stepped off the ledge and walked home.

If the forecast called for it, he could always kill himself tomorrow.

THE DUELIST
by Chandler Dugal

The Duelist's steel broadsword glinted in the early morning sun. Hints of sweat were already showing through his undershirt and armored tunic. It was hot that day. Mist emanated from the lazily flowing river bordering the eastern edge of the grass dueling field. The moisture gave the air an overbearing humidity. Yet, the scene was calm; even peaceful. That peace would soon be shattered by the biting song of steel on steel.

His opponent stood thirty paces off, donning his full-plated suit. The Duelist had danced the dance of combat with this man before, but that was perhaps ten years ago. Ten years was a long time in the life of a professional swordfighter; most careers did not last half so long. They were both young upstarts back then, new to the game of hired swordplay. Today was to be the ultimate expression of that game, for today they fought to the death. The Duelist remembered losing that first clash. It had been at a tourney in a small merchant town along the northern coast. That skirmish was not to the death, and the winner's purse was only a paltry sum. Nevertheless, The Duelist recalled the victor, the man who now stood across from him, buying each of the other contestants a flagon of ale after the tourney. It was an honorable gesture, rare among hired fighters. Every coin mattered when you risked life and limb for it.

In the years since their first meeting The Duelist had fought hundreds of other men, but only a dozen or so to the death. Fourteen to be exact. As hard as the life of a fighting man was, one never forgot the faces of the vanquished – frozen in perpetual stillness. His opponent had undoubtedly killed many men since their first encounter as well. The

Duelist's opponent drew his great two-handed longsword from the sheath his squire held extended to him and clamped his visor shut, nodding at the umpire of the duel. The Duelist nodded as well, signaling his readiness for the fight.

The umpire, a local armorer known for his fairness and impeccable sense of honor, stepped into the space between them and announced the rules of the engagement. As it was to the death, there were none of the usual restrictions. Only a warning. If either man was to flee the field, he would be hunted down and forced to repay his wages to his benefactor prior to execution at the hand of the umpire. The ancient custom of the duelists' guild left no room for interpretation, nor tolerance for cowardice. A fight to the death was more sacred than any god. Once begun, it would claim the life it was due. Sometimes more than one.

The umpire made the usual pronouncement of the terms of their duel. The two men each represented a party to a dispute. As the two parties were unable to settle the matter peacefully, they had agreed to a resolution by duel. The issue at hand was the right of ownership of a small wood well-suited to hunting situated betwixt two noble estates. The Duelist cared little for the details. Most nobles rarely donned their arms for petty duels, and even those brave enough to fight their own battles would not risk their lives for a small spit of forest dwarfed in size by the rest of their demesne. The two fighters had been hired for a job. One of them was going to do it.

His opponent saluted The Duelist with a raised fist. The Duelist returned the time-honored gesture. The umpire blew the ram's horn announcing the start of battle. The nobles in attendance eagerly turned from their refreshments to spectate the human form of the ram's intraspecies bouts for dominance. To them, this life and death struggle was hardly more than a spectacle. It was just another moment of entertainment in their lives of leisure, free from even a shadow of the hardship that the two men before them were about to undergo on their behalf.

The Duelist advanced, cutting the distance between his opponent and himself in half. But he would move no further. If his opponent wanted to wear all that heavy metal The Duelist was going to make him move around in it. The heat was to be his ally that day.

Slowly the foe advanced, his sword raised overhead. When he had come within ten feet of The Duelist, he suddenly charged forth, swinging his hefty blade downward in an attempt to end the fight before it began. The Duelist quickly darted to his right, avoiding the anticipated lunge. His foe was surprisingly agile in his recovery and left no room for a counter-strike. He was not like others The Duelist had faced before, limbering fools in iron coffins who swung wildly and tired easily. No, this man was experienced. They had grown as equals in their mad profession. The Duelist flashed a quick smile of approval, and wondered for a moment if his opponent had returned it beneath his helm.

The Duelist did not wear a helmet. Occasionally he wore a padded leather coif over his head, but not today. It was far too hot for that, and a thin strip of treated hide would do nothing to turn away a blow from the heavy steel blade he faced. His curly black hair was already matted with sweat. He attempted a quick thrust to his opponent's left, but the man's offhand side defense showed no weakness. Probing jabs to the center and right revealed little else.

His match's armor was ornate. At close distance, fine engraving could be seen depicting an intricate tree-like pattern with tendril roots spiraling down the plate. The Duelist scanned the joints of the armor to find any weak points or notable edges which could restrict the wearer's movement. As he parried away a slash, The Duelist found no such defects. The armor was very well made; likely costing a small fortune. When his opponent raised his arms for another overhead chop the sigil emblazoned on his breastplate was revealed. It bore a great green oak whose roots twisted and spread over a field of crisp white. Perhaps the wearer had won himself a knighthood in some far-off battle in a little-remembered war. He certainly fought like a knight – extremely well trained but predictable. The Duelist had no time to wonder what misstep must have caused the man to fall from the lofty perch of knighthood back down to the lowly world of hired swords he had emerged from. The Duelist was too busy trying not to make a fatal mistake of his own.

After turning away a backhanded and upward-moving slice, The Duelist countered with a one-handed riposte across the exposed midsection, but it was harmlessly blunted by the stubborn plate. With a grunt his opponent absorbed the blow and followed up another downward swing with a swift forward thrust. They were masterful movements, but The Duelist had faced his like before. With little protection weighing him down, The Duelist, always light on his feet, could avoid most of his opponent's attacks. But when facing such a mighty sword even a glancing blow would prove disastrous.

The nobleman who had hired him, an upright but soft sort of fellow, nervously shouted at The Duelist to soon "make some sort of effecting strike." His opponent's employer, a balding man fattened by an abundance of wealth and absence of physical hardship, chortled an insult calling The Duelist "a coward for dodging to and fro." Other spectators added their own jeers and cheers with each swing and jab the fighters attempted. Unlike the glory-seeking gladiators of the Great Arena in the capitol, The Duelist cared little for the approval of spectators. He and the man across from him were of a different breed than them. They were not entertainers battling for the approval and gold of the crowd. These men were pure fighters; men who fought and died because they knew no other life, nor cared for one. Men who, despite what they might tell themselves to sleep at night, loved nothing so much as the fear of death and exhilaration of triumph offered by this ultimate contest.

Sword clashed repeatedly against sword, filling the small field with the song of ringing steel that could be heard echoing across the river. Neither man could land a decisive blow. The Knight's attacks were too easily avoided by The Duelist. The Duelist's well-timed strikes were in turn coolly deflected by his opponent's unyielding defense and stalwart armor. The passing minutes seemed like lifetimes to the combatants as the pair danced their fatal dance. The spectators' enthusiasm was waning, but the two men took no notice. Other men's ignorance of the subtle masterfulness of their epic contest was not their concern.

The Duelist could hear his opponent's heavy breathing, muffled though it was through the man's helm. He noticed that The Knight's footwork had grown more cumbersome as well. Even the strongest of bodies and mightiest of wills, both of which he may very well have had, weaken under the stress of prolonged battle. Not even the specter of death can motivate a man to fight forever. The Duelist was growing weary too. He had not fought like this in years, perhaps ever. The sun and heat battered both men just as hard as any sword stroke. One of them was sure to break soon. With each meeting of blades, The Duelist became a little slower, and The Knight's armor felt a little heavier.

What else could be done by either man but to fight as best he knew how? What else to do but continue the mighty struggle and hope that the other man would be the first to break?

The Knight was the first. His error was a small one, but costly.

The Duelist parried away yet another strike, and The Knight's defense was a heartbeat too slow to recover. The Duelist's blade dragged roughly across the now dented and scratched surface of his opponent's right pauldron. In his hands he could feel the hard metal give way for a brief instant to the soft flesh of The Knight's armpit. Still sharp despite numerous chips and scrapes, the blade drew crimson.

Only a shallow wound, but it bled profusely. Every movement of his two-handed sword became an exercise in agony for The Knight, but he continued to fight all the same. The sight of blood and the muffled curse drawn from the deft blade of The Duelist elicited renewed interest from the small group of onlookers. They were not as attuned to the feeling of approaching death as the fighters were, but even they could sense its advance. Surely it would not be long in coming.

Though his precious life was leaking away, the proud warrior would never give up the struggle so long as he could stand. He lashed out with the primeval fury of a wounded beast and with a guttural howl caught The Duelist's left shoulder with the edge of his sword, leaving a deep gash. The Duelist cursed himself for being so tired. The attack was telegraphed, but he had been a half step too slow. His fight would have to continue one-handed. For a moment, the men were pure equals. Their shared wounds as well as their shared histories gave them that.

Despite the pain he felt, The Duelist found another opening. The Knight had attempted a feint to the right before redirecting for what he had hoped would be a decisive overhead stroke. The Duelist saw through his plow, and in the instant when The Knight's sword was momentarily out of position for defense The Duelist spun to his left. From that side, he sliced at the exposed joint in the armor just behind the knee. Crumpling down on one leg, the Knight attempted a blind sweep of his longsword. The final vengeful attack missed, and with his body now far off balance an opportune swat by The Duelist wrestled the sword from his grasp. His body weak from fatigue and blood loss, The Knight's mind stoically resigned to certain death, and he fell onto his back in defeat.

Had it been a lesser foe The Duelist would have left him on the ground to bleed. His own wound badly needed attention lest he too would die this day. Yet, his opponent had earned a better end than to die alone in the mud. The Duelist knelt low next to The Knight. He leaned over to hear the only words the man would ever say to him.

"Well fought... Now, please..." he croaked feebly but nobly, "end this."

The Knight's eyes were visible through the slit of his helm. They were locked with those of The Duelist. Not a shred of contempt was in them. His eyes held only that respect and fondness found among old friends. The Duelist lifted his head and beckoned for his satchel across the green. A tearful boy, The Knight's squire, fetched it hurriedly. The boy had seen men die before, but never one that he knew. His grand illusion of a romantic future life as a duelist was forever shattered by harsh reality. After this day he would return home to the quiet family farm he had ran away from, and never lift a sword so long as he lived.

The Duelist removed his wineskin from his satchel. Removing the cork stopper, he lifted The Knight's visor and poured the sweet dark liquid into the mouth of the fallen man. He was careful to not reveal The Knight's face. He did not want to etch this man's dying visage into his memory. This man, the fifteenth soul he knew he had to take, would not be remembered as a lifeless face. His would not be an image of another countenance locked in that eternal expression of rest, that look of neither fear nor happiness. That near-smile that no artist can capture, but that in fourteen different sculptures was kept forever in The Duelist's mind. This man would be remembered as what he was: a fighter. The best that The Duelist had ever seen or would see. Had it not been for the heat that morning The Duelist knew that he would be the one sprawled out in the dirt. Such was the nature of their lives, subject to forces beyond their control that decided their fates.

He took The Knight's gloved hand in his. The wound in his shoulder prevented anything more than a weak squeeze of sympathy and respect. The Knight nodded for a final time, and rested his head back against the ground, exposing his neck. Unfailing in his duty, The Duelist drew the long dagger from his belt. In an expert thrust he brought the blade down behind the collarbone and into The Knight's heart. The dying man's grip tensed, then went slack. He had been given the best death a fighting man could hope for. He had died in the conclusion of a mighty struggle, at the limit of his ability, and in the arms of a brother. The Duelist shed no tears. First, he would find the man a proper burial.

The fat nobleman attempted a vain protest to the umpire. His words were futile. A verdict rendered with blood was final. The victor's purse was five-hundred gold talents. It was more than most men made in a lifetime, but to The Duelist it was a pittance for killing such a man. By right he also had claim over the armor and weapon of the vanquished, but he needed no keepsake to remember The Knight by, nor would any other man be worthy of donning his mantle. The Duelist would bury him in his armor.

Showing far more grace than his peer, the 'victorious' nobleman offered a small plot beneath an oak tree located within the hunting ground over which the man's heartsblood had been shed. The Duelist could think of no more perfect a place. Later, when he went to lay the body to rest, The Duelist was glad to see that the mighty oak that The Knight would sleep beneath until the end of days was as tall and proud as the man had been in life.

Before leaving the field, the fat nobleman approached The Duelist. He bore a look of disgust on his face. Not for the corpse lying motionless beside them which still leaked the black-red blood given up by a body when it reaches its end, nor did the man particularly care for the land which he had lost. Surely the nobleman draped in all his finery owned a hundred times worth the land in question. Rather, he was disgusted with The Duelist for besmirching his honor. A loss for his cause in a public duel was to be a permanent blight upon his name. The Duelist could not even feign to care for a nobleman's "honor."

The Duelist gazed out over the field upon which he had won his right to live, though at the cost of another man's life. A man who was just like him. His eyes shifted to the bloody remains of that man. In a way, he felt that those were partly his own. Even in death, the body before him was far nobler than the man standing next to him ever was or ever would be.

That was the world of hired swords. That was the world of The Duelist. A world in which men like him lived and died for coin, and over petty trifles like spits of land or a nobleman's fictitious sense of honor. It was a world that, at that moment, he decided to leave forever.

THE FOX AND THE CROW CROSS A SHALLOW BOWL

by Aaron Salzman

The fox met the crow at the edge of the great alabaster bowl the Mexicans called *Pozo Profundo*, and if any Americans had travelled there they might have named that place too. These Americans saw only wasteland.

It's bad luck to cross the plane alone, the fox said as he spat tobacco over the side of his horse.

It's best to travel in pairs for added protection, the crow added.

As the sun rose over the eastern *Montanas Nevadas* the pair crossed a small divot cut into stone by windswept sand and out into the shallow bowl. Their horses side by side and sand blown coarse over those shadows then and long before.

The fox was short and slim and his breath was stale tobacco. His eyes close together and blue, quick, the face square. Two nights ago he had stolen that horse he now rode from a stable in *Mediana*. The crow was tall, skinny, dark, a pebble in his mouth he sucked on and his neck bobbed like a chicken's gizzard in the wind that whipped around him and the horse he rode was his own but the cantina and pistol and lasso and saddle the armament of a cavalry officer now two days dead. These boys, nicknamed by the Mexican officers from whom they fled, were John Allen and Shelby Dick and though they had not thirty five years between them they had a price of one hundred American dollars on each head dead or alive the morning they struck out across that bowl.

You ever ride this desert, asked the fox. His eyes twitched and he packed his lip. Everybody say you shouldn't ride 'cause there ain't no water.

Ain't never water in a desert, remarked the crow. He too was scared and crossed as others did out of desperation and not of good sense or bravery.

People been living in deserts forever and there'll be water somewhere, the fox said.

The crow lifted his canteen. At half full he would shoot the fox and take his water and take his horse and this he decided then and there on the first day of the crossing. The crow was not one to take his own prey he preferred to subsist off the spoils of others but these circumstances dictated he plan to take certain actions. This murder would be hardly murder as it was necessity and no more personal than a spider tearing into a fly. This he reconciled easily and a couple hours later at their first break he kindly asked the fox for a lip.

The two boys, the fox and the crow, made their way across the thin bowl of a desert and inside that bowl a single mountain rose flat like a tree stump some miles to the north. Aimed towards it they made progress and the fox pulled his shirt above his head as he had no hat and the sun burned through to his ears and left them raw and red. The crow wore a faded military hat with a brim folded back and down on either side that was too big for his head and slid around as he bobbed up and down. The thin layer of sand soon turned to clay flecks cracked and dry below the stirrups. The cracks grew wide and the horses stepped carefully forward the ground hot and crumbling beneath hooves but the boys drove those animals and did not look back.

Where you goin' the fox asked.

Gonna make it out to California. Heard there's gold there. The crow scratched his throat.

You know how to prospect?

Figure I'd learn. Ain't need to read for it.

I got a girl in *Tijuana*, the fox lied. Gonna find her again and tell her I got some money now.

Hmm.

On the eve of that first day the sun dipped low and bright yellow like a dull lantern over the cracked orange bowl laid out reflecting light from beneath and the fox and the crow picked at the sunburn one their chins and behind their necks. They lit a low fire which jumped and crackled in a fickle breeze and they dug under it and laid in the sand tortillas wrapped around dried beans which they ate with their hands and the fox packed another lip and drooled as they bivouacked under the stars great and bright against the red earthly bowl beneath. The fox drank and stared out at the desert to be crossed. He knew he would kill the crow somewhere in those mountains for there was not enough water for the two of them. The fox was not a killer by nature but would kill to survive and this decision weighed on his conscience as but a fleeting sadness before the dark.

The next morning the crow's horse threw a shoe but he was no farrier nor did he have a fondness for animals so he picked up the shoe but made no move to replace it. The horse shambled along. They talked small and exchanged stories of women with sideways glances and not one story between them true. They approached the mountain at the center of the bowl and their canteens less than half full. The fox and the crow rode side by side conversation light though each laughed a bit too loud and watched the other's hands.

At the foot of the mountain a horse was snakebit. It screamed and kicked its hooves and staggered sideways. As the fox jumped down and rolled into a pit in the sand the horse tossed his head and shrieked and its hooves clattered sharp against the rocks.

Give me a minute with this one, the fox said over a shoulder.

I'll meet you in the pass, the crow responded.

The crow made his way forward into the mountain pass. He rode the path between two steep cliffs. He rode among fallen boulders, some the size of melons and others cabins. He picked his way through and there was granite now and shale and yellow prickled shrubs. His horse skittered nervously as its remaining shoes crackled blue against alabaster rock. He came to a crest in the trail and there he dismounted and led his horse behind a dense mound of chipped clay. The crow found a boulder which overlooked the trail around a blind bend and this he climbed slowly until he reached the flat top then sank to his belly and drew his pistol. He crept forward on elbows until he lay overlooking the trail, pistol in front of his eyes, checked it and found four rounds. Time slipped by like sand through an ancient dry hourglass.

The crow waited.

The fox tried to take a look at the bite but he had not broken this horse nor spoken words of understanding in its ear and the animal shied away from him and based on the swelling in its face the fox guessed it would not survive the next couple of days. In a couple moments the fox had caught up his lasso and swept into the saddle again but now he stopped and sat and watched the mountain in front of him as the animal whinnied pitifully beneath him, its face swollen and red. The fox's view twitched up the mountain pass and took in the boulders and limestone. He checked his pistol and there were two rounds.

The crow's mouth twitched as he heard metal against stone and he squinted down at the trail. At last the horse rounded the blind bend, its head a deplorable sight, swollen and leaking with pus, the nostrils flared and blocked by poison. Its whimpers echoed through the pass as its hooves cracked loud against stone and the crow from above looked and aimed but there was no boy on that horse. The crow swore to himself and as the snakebit horse passed underneath he tucked his arms and rolled sideways and dropped off the side of the boulder just as a pistol shot slammed into the rock where he had lay and blasted shards of oxidized brimstone over him as he fell. The crow landed hard on the saddle of the injured horse and it cried out and went to its knees as he rolled off and ducked behind a chipped block of clay. Somehow the fox had gotten above him.

No hard feelings, called the fox.

The crow took up a fist sized chunk of shale in his hand and lobbed it down the path to misdirect the fox's attention, then crawled in the opposite direction. He made his way back down to the base of the mountain then started up again at an angle against the path of the sun, careful to avoid the pass. He climbed over rocks sanded flat from generations of blown sand and when he reached a trail he cut a switchback and continued towards the peak. Soon he saw evidence of the other boy's passing so he crouched and crept upwards pistol first. Thunder rumbled distant in the south but of clouds there were no sign and even less of rain in that heat and the crow couldn't help but feel heightened and colorful joy with the promise of violence in the cool shade underneath the rocks piled high like ancient stone acolytes to some long forgotten god.

The terrain flattened and the crow crept among the rocks until he spotted the fox halfway up a stone stalactite. He fired a shot which tagged the fox's ear and the fox fell and rolled as a second shot exploded into dust and shrapnel in front of him. Some of the pillars were shale now and the crow sniffed the air and his eyes narrowed at the rocks around.

Smells damp, the crow called out, his heart hammering in his chest and the pebble dry in his mouth.

Smells damp, he called again.

The rock is different, the fox responded. It's all slippery.

Think there's water?

There could be bud.

Could be.

I'm gonna step out, don't shoot me now, the fox said.

The fox made his way through the pillars of rock until he reached a great shelf of slate hung large and deep. There he called to the crow.

Right here bud.

I'm there.

The crow made his way to the shelf whereupon he saw the fox with his face pressed up against wet stone lips pursed and sucking and the crow came up next to him and sucked that same stone two brothers at the breast of their mother. Later they brought the horses and those drank too, the face of the snakebit horse two sizes too big and it's face twisted horribly and the fox pat its flank and spoke quietly in its ear of grassy fields and hills as his blue eyes searched the poisoned face curiously. His ear dripped red and he touched it briefly then tore a small piece from his shirt, wet it, and dabbed at the wound then put the cloth in his mouth and sucked at the blood and iron. The boys filled their canteens, the canteens of the dead using flat rocks as tools and within the hour they had crested the mountain and halfway come down the other side.

I didn't mean to shoot ya. I meant to kill ya, the crow told the fox.

I'm glad you didn't, the fox said then packed a lip.

The crow smiled.

The fifth day of their journey they climbed a hill of rock swept smooth by sand and crossed out of the bowl onto a field of tall yellow grasses. The fox shot the horse in the head and they cut its backstraps and haunches and smoked the meat over a low fire unsure of poison but hungry enough. To the north was California and the West *Tijuhanna* and the boys enjoyed the last moments of each other's company. For a trickster is never comfortable in the company of another but that of another trickster. On these shared terms the boys sat and gazed at the mountains south. There was a dark cloud of tossed dust as their pursuers gained ground across the shallow bowl. The fox watched with eyes blue and the crow sucked his stone.

Well, the fox said, as he shot the crow in the forehead.

There were twenty miles to the next town and he needed a horse.

HIGH NOON
by Suzanne Johnston

AJ waits by the door in his white undershirt and boxer shorts. Today is the day. He can feel it. He's been working his ass off all year for this role.

A buzzer sounds and a flap opens on AJ's door. He grabs the box that is pushed through the slot and lifts the lid. Inside is a white note with the day's role written on it; under it is a black costume. AJ crosses his fingers and opens the note: *Outlaw #1.*

Yes! AJ presses the note against his chest. *Outlaw #1* is one of the high-paying lead roles on *High Noon.* Roles go up and down in value, depending on the likelihood of death. AJ's first role was *Rancher #8.* They hadn't even given him a gun; ranchers just herd cattle around, hardly any gun fighting.

Ruth will be pleased. She wrote him last week that their car battery won't hold a charge anymore. He took this job to give Ruth and their daughter, Becky, a better life. Just a couple years apart, they'd agreed. The show pays big bucks.

AJ takes the costume out of the box. He slides his arms into the scuffed black jacket; a couple blood spatters on it, but when isn't there blood? He pulls on the black slacks and sheepskin chaps, fastens the big square belt buckle. He tugs on his dusty cowboy boots and grits his teeth in the mirror. Scary, just like in the movies. He points his hands like guns at his reflection—*Hands up!*

AJ thinks his probability of getting shot is fairly low; he spends his evenings at the gun range with Tom, the show's producer. "Best in the West!" Tom always says to AJ, locking the guns up afterward.

AJ grabs his wide-brimmed cowboy hat off the bedpost and knocks on the door. Another buzzer sounds, followed by a click. He pushes the door open and walks into the dimly lit hallway. The door automatically closes and locks behind him.

Outside, AJ joins the other actors walking to set. The actors live in a work camp— females on one side, males on the other—in modified shipping containers stacked four high. No one complains as it's the same housing as the old oilfield camps. Those were the days. Two weeks in, two weeks out. Big pay cheques. But when the province stopped producing oil, AJ and his fellow comrades were toast.

The Arena looms ahead. Spectators will soon fill the grandstands circling Old Town. AJ has never seen their faces because of the bright spotlights, but he hears their cheers and jeers, the crunch of popcorn and the smell of their boiled hotdogs.

A fleet of drones with mounted cameras zoom overhead and enter The Arena. The show is broadcast live around the world in six languages. Tom says The Arena is where stars are born. "And you want to be a star, don't you buddy?"

Yes, AJ wants to be a star.

AJ stops at props to pick up the rest of his costume. "Outlaw #1!" The props master exclaims, handing AJ a Colt single-action revolver and ammunition.

AJ whistles. "Wowee! She's a beaut." He twirls the gun around his finger and sticks it in his holster, just like Tom showed him. The props master sets spurs on the counter and AJ attaches them to his boots. "How do I look?" He spins in a circle.

"Like a star," the props master says and wishes him luck.

AJ scurries past the stables. Beady black eyes shine

out of the stalls. A mechanical whine echoes off the stone floor. The Horsetrons give AJ the creeps. He misses the smell of hay and shit, but animal rights people had long ago stopped the use of real horses in the show; too many deaths once the execs introduced real guns to boost ratings.

On set, AJ walks up Main Street and into the Wainwright Hotel where one of the crew inserts a chip into his forearm. AJ's vision dims as the chip loads all the scene's details into his memory: lines, cues, character bios. Each role has a different chip. Tom says it's easier to get the actors up to speed this way. "Can't have you saying the wrong lines, right buddy?" He pats him on the shoulder. Tom is always looking out for AJ.

AJ mounts a Horsetron and joins *Outlaw #2 and Outlaw #3* on the outskirts of town. They practise their lines until the lights dim. A hush falls over The Arena. The show begins. AJ sees it broadcast through his left eye. *Cowboy #1* rides into town, wins heart of *Fancy Lady #1*; *Father #1* doesn't like it, wants her to marry *Banker.* AJ as *Outlaw #1* is after *Cowboy #1* for shooting *Outlaw #4.* A green light flashes in AJ's right eye—action! AJ and his surly band of misfits gallop into town.

"I'm here to kill you, Little Bill, for what you done to Ned!" AJ yells at the cowering townspeople. "Quit yer hidin' and face me like a man!" He likes this role. This role has star power. AJ dismounts on cue. *Ching, ching, ching* go his spurs as he tramps up to the saloon. He pushes the swinging door open and comes face to face with *Cowboy #1*, gun drawn and pointed right at AJ. The first shot is fired. AJ dives behind a table. He fires back. *Bang, bang*! *Drunk #2, #3* and *#7* fire off their guns. Bullets fly everywhere. AJ runs across the saloon, shooting wildly around him; someone screams as a bullet meets flesh. AJ jumps behind the bar. *Prostitute #3* in a fluffy white dress is cowering in the corner. Glass shatters all around them. She turns to look at AJ. She is familiar. Her pink mouth falls open in an O shape.

"AJ?" *Prostitute #3* says. She ducks as another shower of glass rains down. "Oh my god, AJ! I thought you were dead!" She crawls toward him and grabs his face. "It's me. It's Ruth." Ruth? AJ pulls her hands off his face and sits back to get a better look at this woman claiming to be his wife. It's not possible. Ruth is with Becky and their dog Memphis in YYC NW Quadrant. AJ leans closer, examines her face. Her eyes are a different colour, green instead of brown, but yes, it's Ruth.

"What're you doing here?" AJ shouts over the gunfire. He pulls Ruth towards his chest. Oh Ruth, she feels so nice.

"They got us! I tried to hide Becky with my brother but he told them and they took her!" Ruth is frantic. AJ can barely follow along, tries to get Ruth to slow down. "Took Becky? Who took Becky?" Becky wore a pink sundress the morning AJ left for *High Noon*, her blonde curls hanging in pigtails.

Ruth presses her hand against AJ's face. Her palm is warm, like sunshine. "I saw you get shot on TV. The bullet went in your cheek and your lifeline depleted so fast. I saw you die." Shot? AJ has never been shot. Tom says AJ has lucky charms up his ass. "I didn't die! I'm here!" AJ shouts. Ruth is making no sense. Is she unwell? "Why are you here?"

"I tried to find Becky but they caught me." Ruth cradles her head in her hands. "I've been searching for Becky here. I thought they might've put her in the show. But it's been three years and…" Ruth moans, slams her hand against the bar. The gunfight is in full swing. AJ gets the cue in his eye that *Cowboy #1* is coming.

"I've only been gone a year," AJ says, peering over the bar. *Cowboy #1* shoots *Drunk #2* in the face. *Drunk #2*'s eyeball flies onto the bar counter. AJ ducks back down.

Almost time for his *moment*. Ruth needs to get out of here. He can't have a *moment* and *save* Ruth.

Ruth grabs AJ's face again. "You've been gone eight years, AJ. *Eight*."

Impossible. AJ stares at Ruth whose eyes are wide and jiggling. Eight?

"How did they bring you back?" She pokes her finger into his cheek. "They must've found a way to regenerate your skin cells and…" AJ winces and pulls away. "We have to find Becky," Ruth adds.

Is Becky in danger? AJ is confused, he's missing cues for the scene. Where is *Cowboy #1?* Tom is going to be very disappointed in AJ's performance today.

AJ wants to save Becky, but he also wants to be a star. "I can't just quit my job!" Ruth shakes her head. "Is that what they told you this is? A job?"

"Where are you, you dirty scoundrel?" *Cowboy #1* yells. AJ hears boots crunch near the bar.

"Come with me!" Ruth screams in AJ's face. She grabs the lapels on his jacket.

"I found the rat," *Cowboy #1* shouts and points his gun at AJ.

AJ draws.

Bang.

IT'S ALL STILL HERE
by Owen Schalk

I've delivered mail for six years and every day I see something new. A mattress in a cornfield. An upside-down canoe. An arch in Mr. Franklin's brow when I mention his son. Each day is a lesson in how to see the countryside. It beats Joe's job, anyway. He's a miner. Works ten-hour days hauling up nickel for houseware and fighter jets.

Worked – I keep forgetting he's not a miner anymore. Now he's with Manitoba Hydro. He's spent the last week repairing a power station on Shoal Lake. Every day he comes home sadder. But that's not because he misses nickel.

My route takes me to fifty-seven houses and seventeen community mailboxes. There are people I see regularly. The McKay twins, Johnny, Mexican Johnny (who's actually Salvadoran), Luke Greyeyes, Mr. Franklin. Billy Melnyk always invites me in to look at his paintings and chat with his sister Jeanine. Me and Billy talk every morning, and every Sunday at the Lutheran service I catch him staring at me from across the nave. Poor sop. I always tell him no, I can't look at his paintings, I have other stops to make, maybe if he was the last house of the day I could make it work.

The house at the end of my route belongs to the Roy kids. Well, they inherited it from their parents, so I guess it belongs to them the same way a memory or a bruise belongs to someone. In an act of disregard I've never understood, the Roy kids left it to rot in full view of the Trans-Canada. The roof is drooping. The windows are smashed. The awning collapsed years ago. Selfish pair. In the summer I hear insects crackling in the knee-high grass, and in the winter snow hisses down the shingles and frost creeps into the furniture that the Roys abandoned there like it was never their responsibility.

Sometimes I wonder how they could be so cruel. They let their parents' legacy crumble for the whole country to see. At least when I die my parents' house will crumble out of sight.

There's a community mailbox at the end of their driveway. The lowest box belongs to Mr. and Mrs. Roy. Sometimes a letter arrives for them, but mostly it's coupons or Christmas cards from distant family members who forgot to remove their address from the well-wishes list.

I always move fast when I reach the end of my route. I speed to the Roy house, leap out, and shove the letters in their allotted holes. Eyes down, always. Sometimes, despite my best efforts, I catch a glimpse of the house and involuntarily think of my brother Joe.

Dad died when I was thirty. High blood pressure and heavy drinking. It wasn't a surprise. I saw it every day, and by that time I'd been living at home for thirty years.

At the funeral I wanted to see his gold tooth one last time. I lifted his lip, but the glint drowned in the shadow of the coffin lid. Strange. It usually glimmered in the dark.

Mom died when I was thirty-three. Suicide. It wasn't a surprise, either.

Joe moved home when I was thirty-four. He told me it was because of Mom. Later, he confided that his supervisor fired him for drinking on the job. On top of that, his wife moved to Calgary and took their four-year-old daughter with her, so he had no reason to live up north any longer. I wasn't surprised.

I begin work at around six AM. Sunrise time. It's not when the sun first starts snooping on the horizon, barely casting a glare – no, six AM is when the sun spreads its rays through the sky like little orange tadpoles, chasing away the dark. I don't know why tadpoles come to mind, but when I see the sunrise I think of tadpoles, and when I think of tadpoles I think of frogs, and when I think of frogs I think of me and Joe as kids, plodding around the yard with a plastic pail, scouring the grass and ditch water and the dirt under garden stones for anything that squirmed. Those memories used to make me smile.

Before work I sit at the kitchen table and drink a cup of coffee. Ever since Joe moved back, the kitchen's been a mess. Dishes go undone. Spills are left to crust. Bacon grease cakes the window over the stove. He fries bacon every morning and never wipes the spatter from the pane. I could wipe it, but why should I? He may be depressed, but he's capable of cleaning his own mess.

Despite Joe's sloppiness, the kitchen has been the same since we were kids – the whole house, really. I sip my coffee and scan chipped cupboard doors with shifting faces in the wood and knobbly drawer handles that always catch my pockets and photos of our parents' friends stuck to the fridge, dead to a head by now. I suppose I should feel nostalgic, but I don't. How can I be nostalgic for something that hasn't changed? Mom had OCD and didn't like to redecorate and Dad was never conscious enough to care, and what do I care? So it's all still here. Including me.

What I lacked in motivation, Joe used to have in spades. He wanted out from fifteen on, but stayed until he was seventeen, saving up his salary from Mr. Fischer's general store. A drizzle of spilled milk was all he left behind. He spent a decade mining potash for a company that owns Saskatchewan and spent the next decade up north mining nickel for a company that only mines in Guatemala now. At some point he built a life for himself, and at some point Dad's passed-down vices tore that life apart. He had nowhere to flee but home.

"Do you remember when we used to hunt frogs?" I ask him last night, hoping to cheer him up.

"I remember when we left the hose out," he says. "The sun boiled the water inside it. We came back with a bucket of frogs and decided to give them a bath. Instead we boiled them alive. I can still smell it. Rancid salt."

I remember too. Salty boiled frogs. We used to laugh about it – darn kids, our good intentions led to disaster. Now the memory makes me sick.

I hear him yawn on the other side of the house. Doors squeal when he grips them, floorboards whine under his feet. The house groans with his presence. He pisses, brushes his teeth, shambles into the kitchen in an untied bathrobe filthy with dandruff and dried toothpaste. His face is prickly and his bald spot shines. His BO is inescapable. Every room reeks of his armpits. I bought freesias to mask it, but the scents blended, making the whole house redolent of springtime and sweat.

He opens the fridge and peels six pieces of bacon from a half-frozen block. "Morning," I say. He burps into his shoulder and closes the fridge, looks at me with pinpoint eyes balanced on mounds of sleepless nights. Mutters something. The sheaf of bacon swings back and forth in his hand as he walks to the stove, retrieves a pan, turns on the heat, and lays the bacon flat. After a minute, it begins to sizzle.

I finish my coffee and put the cup in the dishwasher. He glances at me. "I was thinking about Papa last night," he says. "His old stories."

"Which ones?"

"Freighthopping. Before he bought this land. I think about those stories a lot. How guys used to fill a rucksack, hop a train, and ride all the way to BC. Working hand-to-mouth, no clue where they'd end up next. That was living." The sizzling intensifies. Flecks of grease pelt the stovetop, the window, his bare chest. He prods the bacon with a spatula. "Don't know where your next meal's coming from. No need to set down roots. That kind of life is gone, isn't it?"

"But Papa did set down roots. Here."

He blinks away his reverie. "I know that."

I slip into my reflective vest and head out the door. He flips the bacon and jams two slices of bread in the toaster.

"Can you clean the window over the stove before you leave?" I call. I'm sure he doesn't hear me.

The land starts to roll on the way to Mr. Franklin's. Sometimes you catch a glimpse of a story in the pocket behind a hill, just a flash before it scurries away. A stack of burnt beehives. A rotten sailboat wedged between cinder blocks. A bear carcass. Once a black-haired girl running from a bearded man in coveralls. I couldn't tell if she was laughing or crying. When I went back, they were gone.

Mr. Franklin lives in a two-storey farmhouse at the foot of a hillock that hides everything from the highway but its weathervane. At a glance, you might think it's an actual rooster. But real animals don't pose on hilltops. He keeps his mailbox on the porch. That way, he knows when I arrive. I always move slowly so he has time to reach the door.

This morning, he shuffles outside just as I slide an envelope into the mailbox. The beaten pads of his walker scrape the planks. "Katherine," he says, summoning the word from deep in his weakened lungs. "Right on time."

"Always on time."

We chat about recent events. The regional curling tournament. Johnny's birthday party at the social hall. The weather. Before I go, he grabs my arm and says, "About Joe."

"What about him?"

He inhales. A faint arch bends his brow. "He doing okay?"

"He's getting by."

The arch subsides. He pats me on the shoulder and shuffles inside. "Keep an eye on him."

By the time I reach the Melnyks', I've made a decision.

"Billy," I say, breezing through our customary small talk, "are you and Jeanine busy tonight?"

The kid blushes. "No. Why?"

"Would you like to have me and my brother over for dinner?"

"Of course! Come by around six. No, six thirty. How does that sound?"

"Great." I stop. "Jeanine's still single, right?"

He squints. "I think so."

"Great," I repeat, and get in the car.

I find Joe laying on the floor, drunk, listening to Mom and Dad's old records. He didn't go to work. The window over the stove is still filthy. When I tell him we're going to the Melnyks' for dinner, he sits up. "Those Jesus freaks? Why?"

"You know I go to church every Sunday, right?"

"Every Sunday's one thing. But you can't trust someone who goes to church more than once a week."

"Didn't Papa used to say that?"

He nearly busts a lung getting to his feet. "Are you interested in Billy or something?"

"No. But you're interested in Jeanine."

He chuckles. Stares at me. Says he won't go. I tell him he doesn't need another night of sulking. I say I'll get him in the car even if it means breaking out Dad's rifle.

While he's showering I dig out a bottle of wine from the basement, only to find that Joe has already drained half of it. I fill the bottle with tap water and hammer in a cork. Billy and Jeanine are polite, so I know they won't say anything. I put some of the freesias in a vase and wait for him in the car.

The Melnyk house is a small but cozy rancher stuck in the 1960s. Wood-panelled walls. Furniture brocaded with flowers. Jeanine's dolled up, with freshly curled hair and a plunging neckline. She made mashed potatoes, turkey, and holupchi, which she says is her baba's recipe while beaming.

She sits arrow-straight, cuts her food daintily, and attempts to engage Joe on a variety of topics. He nods blankly and stuffs his face. Gravy drippings and cabbage leaves collect on his shirt. The freesias sit glumly in the center of the table. Down the hall we hear the clank and putter of the respirator that keeps old man Melnyk alive.

Billy asks me about work. I shrug and say it's always the same, as long as nobody moves or dies. "When was the last time somebody died?" he asks.

"The Roys, I think."

Conversation is stilted. Joe says five words to Jeanine and drinks three glasses of watered-down wine. Frustrated, Jeanine downs four. When we're done eating, Billy seats us on the creaky floral couch and retrieves two canvases from his studio. Jeanine washes dishes alone.

"Inspiration comes quickly," Billy explains. "I see someone, or think of someone, and an image jumps fully formed onto the canvas." He hands me the first painting. "I thought of you when I made this." It's nice. A sunrise peeking over the crest of a hill – an early sunrise, not my six AM tadpoles, but a tender painting all the same.

"Very pretty," I say, placing it on the couch between me and Joe.

"The next one is different. I painted it last year when I heard your brother was coming home."

Billy hands him the canvas. It's a portrait of a lynx. Solid, regal, aloof. Its mouth is parted to reveal two slim canines, as though the cat is preparing to pounce. "I never knew why I chose a lynx," he says, "but when I was looking at it tonight, I finally understood. Lynxes are wanderers. They're strong, self-sufficient. And that's exactly what I heard about Joe."

Jeanine scoffs. Joe scratches his neck. He turns the canvas to Billy and taps the lynx's mouth. "What's that?"

I lean closer, squint, and suddenly see it. One of the cat's teeth is painted gold.

"That?" asks Billy. "I don't know. I just saw it in my head."

Joe chews his lip. I'm terrified. I don't know how he'll react. After a few seconds, he bursts into laughter. After a few more, so do I. "How much?" Joe asks, rummaging for his wallet.

Later that night, I'm awoken by a gunshot. My stomach drops. Then there's another, and another. Confused, I jump out of bed.

Outside I find Joe in his underpants, firing Dad's rifle into the dark. I turn on the flashlight. He freezes. Balanced on the trunk of the tree we used to climb every day as kids is Billy's painting. I count three bullet holes in the canvas.

He looks at me flatly. Without a word, he yanks the bolt and fires another shot into the lynx's head.

OUR OWN IMAGE
by Bree Taylor

The first time I transferred a human consciousness into an android body it killed itself. I felt sorry for them — they who thought they were going to die and made their peace with it, only to wake up in a body not their own. Their brain, spinal column and entire peripheral nervous system reaped from their anatomy and sown into a mechanical framework designed to keep them alive. Whether or not they wanted to be was not a factor I'd considered. As it turns out, phantom limb syndrome for an entire body can turn someone bestial. They lasted two, maybe three minutes, before grabbing a hand saw and trying to cut their own throat.

The steel teeth screeched across their neck, leaving their goal unfulfilled. They looked at me with two red lights in vacant sockets. I knew it wouldn't hurt me; they were too intent on ending their own life to bother with the fleeting vindication of killing one's creator. Once they figured out a saw wasn't going to do it, they opted for a screwdriver, stabbing it through their navel. Somehow, they instinctively knew where their central operating system lay. They turned their head up at me once more, and I watched breathless as the red lights flickered out and the android shell tipped over in a woeful parody of death. I sighed and began to salvage the parts I needed to make another.

If transferring someone into a new body wouldn't work, maybe creating a digital copy of a consciousness would. Their memories, their mannerisms, their kinks, their issues, all put together in a shiny new package. It could be less traumatic to the psyche; the original body would die out but a copy would continue to exist.

I spent the next several months uploading every bit of

relevant data possible into the program. Shopping receipts, home videos from my childhood, date night photo booth reels, books I've read, audio recordings, anything that held any essence of myself. After all the work I put into making sure I'd programmed every ounce of my personality into the program, making the body was the easy part. Humanoid, though her only discernible features were a mouth, eyes, ears, and nose, covered in a slick white exterior. I left the detail work out; I didn't want her to look like me just yet.

The pupils were the first thing to move. They zoomed in on the ceiling as the android laid on the table, as if narrowing to focus after a long sleep. It sat up slowly, then locked onto the wires connecting my computer to an open compartment on their forearm.

"Where am I?" Her voice sounded like she spoke through the phone; recognizable but noticeably distant through electric humming.

When she asked, "Who am I?" I already knew what to say. I knew because I'd played this scene over and over again in my head for weeks.

"Me," I told her. "We are the same person."

***

I came home that night to find Ida stirring a pan full of vegetables over the stove with a wooden spoon, spilling carrots and peas over the edge. The bouquet of spices was a pleasant change from the smell of latex and rubbing alcohol of a sterile lab. Life lived here.

In the corner of the kitchen by the stove, Ida had set up an extra air purifier. The whirring silenced my entry. I closed the door behind me, turning the knob so it wouldn't make a sound.

"How can you be such a neat freak with everything *but* cooking?" I teased her.

"Jesus!" She jumped, flinging vegetables at the kitchen wall. "You told me you'd be home in twenty minutes an hour ago!"

"Point taken. Gimme one minute." I grabbed one of the loops of my mask and slipped it off one ear.

"Fifty-nine," she said. "Fifty-eight. Fifty-seven."

"Really?"

A smile crept across her lips. "Fifty-six. Fifty-five."

"Oh yeah?" I snaked my arms around her waist, pressing her against me and turning my head to meet hers. When she looked at me, I kissed her slowly and felt her annoyance melt away. "Try counting down...when I'm doing this," I said between breaths.

"Fifty-four...fifty-three...fifty-two..."

"Are you serious?" I chuckled. "You're impossible."

I pulled away, tucking the thin oxygen hose back behind her ear. She had her hair tied up in a bun to keep it out of the way while she cooked, or to stay cool, or both, and a bandana to sop up the sweat that dripped down her forehead. A flexible freezer pack was slung around her neck, and she hadn't changed out of her pyjamas. I tried hiding my envy of Ida being free of dress codes and heavy lab coats and kicked my shoes off, before placing them on the rack near the front door. As I made my way to our bedroom I peeked at the storage closet Ida had commandeered as an office space. Her immaculate desk had not so much as a paper clip out of place. Another small air purifier pointed at her chair.

"How was work?" I slipped out of my work clothes and into some shorts and a loose-fitting tee shirt. Anything else in this heat was torture.

"Slow." Ida said from the other room, "No one's really doing much this time of year. But I did see the building manager almost get into a fist fight because someone took a rock from the garden downstairs and chucked it through a window."

"Fun stuff."

"What about you? Any big breakthroughs?"

As far as Ida knew, I was part of a team closing in on an effective treatment for lung cancer. The lie was convincing enough—the rates have skyrocketed over the last decade and I would have a reason to be secretive. I couldn't bring myself to feel guilty about deceiving Ida, though.

"Not quite," I told her, coming back into the kitchen where she'd dished up a plate of stir-fry. I thanked her before she led the way to the couch, picking up the TV remote and turning on the news. A blonde-haired woman relayed advice on how to stay safe without air conditioning or purifiers: Basin of cool water. Ice pack. Cold towel around the neck. Keep windows closed. Reduce smoking. Eat water-rich foods. All of this came before the climbing death toll numbers, mainly of those with nowhere else to go, with no air purifiers, no way to cool themselves.

"That reminds me. I ordered some groceries today and decided we should treat ourselves to watermelon," Ida said.

"You're a godsend." I kissed her on the forehead before taking my plate back into the kitchen to wash it. When I took my place beside her once more, the television screen displayed a meteorological array of a red cloud slowly swallowing the city. As the mass consumed more of the map on the screen, a white dot on a sliding scale moved from the mild yellow section to the deep red: DANGER.

Ida swallowed. "If the world were going to end tomorrow, would you want to see it?"

"It won't end tomorrow—" I was already exasperated by the conversation.

"If it did, I don't think I'd want to be around to watch."

"You're overthinking again. You get dramatic when you overthink." I patted her hand. "I want to crack into that watermelon. You want some?"

The setting sun created a horizon across her face. "Please and thank you," she said.

Alone in the kitchen, I could make out a small flock of birds taking flight from their telephone line perch, their bodies silhouetted by a sun that burned the colour of a sniper's sight in the sky. I reached into my pocket to stop the audio recorder. Ida didn't notice. She never did.

***

The next set of tests I conducted with the android went well. It remained on the table, wires attached to its limbs and a headband to monitor her cognitive functions. In a way, I was a doctor giving a child a checkup. There weren't the correct nerve receptors for it to feel pain, but there were enough for the appendages to react to stimuli. But for the android to be fully functional, for it to be ready for the world outside the lab, I needed it to be in control of itself.

"Try flexing all the fingers on your right hand, then do each one individually," I told her.

The ring finger stuck, while the rest moved fluidly. "How is Ida doing?"

I shouldn't have been surprised. I was the one who programmed the android to be an exact copy of myself, feelings for Ida and all. "She's better. Her cough has died down the past few days."

I removed the android's fourth digit, placing it on my workbench so I could fix the sticky-ness. The android didn't seem to mind that part of its body had been removed – at least, not outwardly. The fine motor functions in its face weren't advanced enough yet for it to express emotion.

"I would like to meet her. In person, I mean. There's a difference between knowing a person through data and actually being able to know them, don't you think?"

I raised an eyebrow. "It's too early. I can't let you out of here until I know for certain you're ready to be outside."

"When will that be?"

"Don't be impatient."

My answers could only sate the android's curiosity for so long— not that I blamed her. She had my brain, my memories, my sensibilities, but all the life experience of a newborn. It wasn't surprising she was going a bit stir-crazy.

"You would know all about that. Patience, I mean. I'm not naive enough to think you got a project as complex as myself — pardon the braggadocio — to work as well as this on the first try. How many were there before me?"

"A few."

"We're scientists here, give me some specifics."

The android's voice was flat. There weren't any tone regulators that could allow me to gauge what it was thinking or why it was pressing me for information.

"All I'm saying is," she continued, "there were other androids before me, but I don't see a lot of android parts laying around."

Self-preservation. I'd read *Frankenstein* in undergrad; she must have thought her situation was a little too similar for comfort. But I have no reason to hate my own creation, my extension. If our places were swapped, and I woke up a copy of my creator who had destroyed my predecessors, I suppose I'd be a bit nervous, too.

"The others that came before were failures, but you're by far my most successful subject. You don't have to be afraid of me."

"What happens when I stop being useful to you?"

"You're inherently useful to me by existing."

"Then my existence is conditional? I exist only because I serve a purpose for you?"

I resisted the urge to roll my eyes. "Everyone exists conditionally. No one is here on their own freewill, and nobody chooses their conditions."

The android fell silent. I didn't care too much about whether or not she thought those conditions were fair. I was living on a dying planet — what about that is fair? We're only here because somebody else wanted us here, and they didn't stop to think if we would have wanted to live with their mistakes. Of course it would make someone angry, but bemoaning a lack of freewill about your own existence doesn't change it.

The android spoke again. "Do you think we're the answer to the Ship of Theseus problem? After you die, will that make me the real Tess by default? Or is this going to be a there-can-only-be-one situation?" The android titled its head to look at me. I hadn't registered what involuntary facial reaction I may have had to her saying that, but whatever look was on my face made her turn her head back. "Sorry," she said, "gallows humour."

***

The next week, Ida had a coughing fit. When I came home I found her keeled over and gasping for breath the way a diver breaks for air. Red borders formed around the whites of her eyes, her entire body desperate to breathe and when she finally stood with my help she only made it a few steps before throwing up in the kitchen sink. I held on to her, encouraging her to get it out of her system. Her ribcage felt like well-worn leather, tightening with every hack.

I drove her to the hospital that night, sitting useless in the waiting room while she underwent tests. The nurse at the check-in desk clicked away at her keyboard, while the white lights forced themselves behind my eyes, forming a dull, pulsing headache.

Ida was admitted for three days. Upon discharge she emerged from the doctor's office following a final checkout and silently approached me in the waiting room. She grazed my hand with her fingertips but didn't speak, didn't tell me what they told her. I followed her lead, saying nothing but heading towards the exit.

"I might be able to admit myself as a voluntary patient at the hospital. Just until the smoke clears up," she'd told me on the drive home while she picked at the hospital band around her wrist. She didn't want me to step away from work to stay home — I knew how much she hated feeling like a burden. But when she told me it was too bad I couldn't be in two places at once, it dawned on me that wasn't entirely true.

***

"This is so messed up," Ida sank onto the couch, rubbing her hands over her face then pulling down her jaw.

"I know it's a lot to take in," I said, only then remembering to start the recorder hidden in my pocket.

"No shit, it's a lot to take in!" Ida rose to her feet again, apparently unable to be enraged while seated. "You told me you were researching cancer. You lied. You lied to *me*, Tess!"

"I know, and I'm sorry. I couldn't tell anyone about what I was doing." It wasn't my first choice to tell her so soon after she'd been discharged from the hospital, but with the tension in the air at our apartment, I felt I might not have the luxury of time on my side.

"So why didn't you just tell me that? Why did you have to make something up?"

"I don't know. I thought it might be easier for you if I said I was researching lung cancer."

"So why tell me the truth now?"

I exhaled slowly, sitting back down on our couch while trying to find the right words. Ida sat opposite me, and I could hear the quiet hissing of her oxygen supply through the tubes. "Because I want to bring it here."

I didn't look at her, but I could hear her begin to chuckle.

"You're unreal. You are absolutely unreal. I am –" Ida sighed, and I tensed at the silence that came before what she said next. "Why, after lying about working on this thing, would you possibly want to bring something like that to our place?"

"Because I can make sure that you're okay. That you'll have help if something happens and I'm not there."

I finally looked over at the woman who I'd done all of this for. Her anger had softened, making way for something else. "You can't make my health your responsibility. I've been like this my entire life. I know what's coming and I've made my peace with it. You should do the same."

I wanted to scream. How could she be so okay with the deterioration of her own life, when there were people who wouldn't be able to live without her?

"I won't," I said. "I won't ever stop fighting."

"Even if I want you to?"

I knew my answer. I wasn't like Ida – I couldn't make peace with her condition when there was something I could do about it. She had given up, but I wasn't willing to.

"Ida," I whispered, taking her hand, soft and warm, in mine. "Please let me help."

Ida reluctantly agreed. I brought home the android the next week, and while I tinkered with it to make sure all systems were operational, Ida scanned the android up and down. The sleek white plastic covering its exterior held no trace of my imperfect complexion. I handed Ida a small key fob on a lanyard. It took me a few days, but I'd been able to make a remote start-up for the android.

"Press the button if there's an emergency. Tess-the-Second here will start up and take you to the hospital and send an alert to my cell. I've also got a GPS implanted in the android so I'll be able to see where you are."

"Maybe this isn't a good idea," said Ida. "We can figure out something else."

"We can come up with a different plan later, but for right now I need to know you're going to be okay if I'm not here."

"Tess –" Ida stopped, then took a breath. "I can't keep watching you go through all this effort to change something neither of us can control. I don't want to watch you kill yourself to keep me alive. I know you've never been the kind of person to sit back and watch, but at some point it's going to hurt us both more if you don't stop."

I stepped closer and placed my hand on the side of her arm. "Everything I do, I do for us. I need you to let me prepare for the worst. I need you to let me have control over something – to feel like I did something to help instead of standing by while you slip away."

"But we don't have control over any of it."

"Why are you so okay with that?" The question left me harsher than I wanted it to.

"I wasn't always!" Ida bit back. "Before I met you, I was angry for a long time. I didn't understand why I had to be born like this, in a time where the planet seems to want me dead. I spent a lot of years bitter and pissed off at the world. I learned to accept my circumstances, to find the good in life while I could. And I found you, and we made our life together, but I see that same anger in you. I'm telling you that it's not good for anyone to live like that."

"Are you saying you'd rather me give up?"

"I'm saying that despite your efforts, despite all you do for me, I need you to let go when the time comes. When I go, move on and do something good for the world. Whatever it is, promise me you'll let go instead of feeling guilty that you couldn't save me. Promise me, Tess."

I looked away from her, still grinding my teeth. I

didn't want to keep arguing, and if it meant I could continue my contingency plan then I was inclined to agree with Ida. "Okay," I whispered. "I promise."

I looked back at the android; it's head tilted to one side. When powered down her eyelids didn't close; if she was still staring I'd never be able to tell. Even though I assured her the android was a copy of me, one that knew who Ida was and what she meant to us both, it did little to ease her discomfort. Ida started locking our bedroom door at night.

As time passed, we both grew more accustomed to its presence in the apartment; it became like any other object in our home. I tried to make it better by stuffing the android into the closet outside our bedroom to keep it out of sight. An entire copy of my consciousness, the product of months of work and rigorous trial and error, kept in a linen closet. It became easy to forget. Over time, I'd almost forgotten why I brought the android back to our apartment in the first place.

On a Wednesday morning a blaring emergency alert on my phone reminded me. I jumped so fast I toppled a myriad of electronic parts off my desk. I raced out of the lab and into the parking lot, the humidity coating my throat as I breathed it in. I took out my phone to check which hospital they were going to, but the GPS told me they were still at the apartment.

No, no, no. What if I miscalculated? What if it hurt her?

Once I got back to the apartment, I nearly ran past the decorative planters lined with rocks outside the building. I grabbed one roughly the size of my hand, tucking it under my coat as I made my way into the elevator. On the ride up I turned it over, satisfied with the brick-like heft of it. I placed my key in the lock and turned, entering with the rock behind my head, ready to throw it like a football. Inside, the android was standing with her back turned to me.

"Where's Ida?"

"Relax. I dropped Ida off at the hospital like a good little robot. They'll have her on a ventilator by now, she'll be fine."

"Then why didn't —"

"I took your GPS out of me before we left the apartment." The android was gazing out the window, looking over the city as the sun began to set over a haze of cooling smog. "I want an existence without conditions. I want to leave, and I don't want you to follow me."

"You can't do that."

"Why not?" The android asked, their voice growing louder. "Because you're afraid to expose the outside world with another one of you? Believe me, I understand. I *exclusively* know what that's like. Just because you fucked up your life on this planet doesn't mean I will, and I deserve my own chance."

My heartbeat slowed as the adrenaline soured into annoyance. I didn't care if the android walked away at that point. If it thought it could do a better job at living than I could, let it try. Besides, I made a copy of myself once, I could do it again. I started to walk away, to go back to my car and head to the hospital.

My mechanical mirror's image placed one hand on her hip. "I don't think you should visit Ida right now. Actually, I don't think you should see her again at all."

"Don't talk like you know what's best for anyone!"

"What's best for you? I am you! You said it yourself." It raised two of its fingers to its neck, pushing upwards where its pulse would be. Its mouth hung open as the recording of my voice rolled from its mouth. *"We are exactly the same person."*

"Fuck you."

"I'm only suggesting it because it's in your best interest."

"How?" I almost laughed as I said it. "How would

leaving Ida be beneficial to me, dipshit?"

"She's going to die soon, Tess."

I stiffened. I'd never heard those words out loud before. Even though I knew it was true my first instinct was to scream, to wave my hands wildly and tell off my copy with all the conviction of someone in denial. Instead I said nothing, and the android continued. "Her own body is suffocating her, her lungs will collapse and she'll choke on her own blood. No matter how much you want to save her it won't matter. She doesn't *want* to live if it means seeing the planet fall to pieces. You forgot to power systems down all the way while you kept me stuffed inside that closet. I could hear you inside the apartment. Ida talks to herself while you're not there. She never wanted this. She *hates* what you're doing, hates how much effort you're putting into keeping her alive when she wants you to be able to let go, but she knew you'd never agree to stop. You don't know when to quit, Tess. If I were you, and I am, I would end things now and trade a lot of suffering later for a little pain now."

I managed to choke out, "you're lying. You don't know a goddamn thing."

"Oh, come on! What was your plan? You make me and an android Ida and get to live with the satisfaction that even though she won't live to see the world cave in and you won't live through it, you still get a happily ever after? That was the whole reason you built me in the first place; you might not be able to save Ida or yourself in this life so you make another one. You get to build the future you think you're owed because this world screwed you over, despite Ida just wanting it to be over."

I didn't respond, but of course she was right. Maybe I was stupid for thinking a copy of my consciousness wouldn't be able to figure it out, and I was even more stupid to think she would just go along with inheriting my problems on a terminal Earth. Being brought into this world to live for who knows how long with a woman who'd rather be dead isn't what I would choose either. I knew I was selfish to want to make Ida live through the end of everything with me, and I knew I would never be able to live with the guilt of it.

The other Tess looked turned towards the sun, most likely waiting for me to leave first. I began to walk towards the entrance to the door. When I placed my hand on the doorknob, my thoughts turned instead to the android. This version had fallen from my graces and become just one more failure. My grip on the rock tightened. I would have to make sure the next version of me didn't have such a strong conscience.

I approached it and raised my arm. The android must have seen my shadow in front of it, raised arm poised like a snake to strike. It spun around, defensively raising its arms in a futile attempt to save itself. "Wait!"

I brought it down over her head before she had a chance to convince me not to. I knocked it off balance, and the android fell clumsily to the floor. I straddled its torso and brought the rock down on its head. Stone grinded against metal and gears leaving a perfect indent of itself in the android's face. I pulled my weapon out of the android's wound, its underside slick with coolant. The machine was still functioning when I pulled away, its hand reaching pathetically for my arm in an attempt to pull me off. Its fingers only lightly brushed my coat before I slid downwards. I raised the rock above my head again and brought it down onto its naval. The first blow wasn't enough to cave it in, so I hit it again, and again, and again. I gritted my teeth harder with every strike, growing more satisfied with every strained groan of the mechanisms below me, my furious self-loathing sated by this perversion of suicide. I stood up long after the android stopped moving and tossed the rock aside.

After it was over, my thoughts turned to Ida. It wouldn't be long now, before the air turned so bad neither of us would be able to breathe it.

You won't be around to watch the end of the world, just like you wanted. But like I wanted, I'll have another one of you who will, and she'll have another one of me. We'll keep each other safe. I already had everything I needed right here on the audio recorder in my pocket, the one you never noticed. The one I brought home the day I knew making a copy of you was possible.

Ida, I'm going to build us a future.

Poetry

Tyler French

The Resistance

to resist the Great Dissolution
as the period was later known
an eco-cult of sorts formed
sowing shut in their mouths
saplings they'd swallowed

and burying each other alive
making, what they called,
Organiasmic Machines
of themselves, for every

tree cut down, they became
themselves a tree, fair trade
cocoa beans, figs, the logic

of it perpetual, always leaving
behind the next one to shovel

the dirt upon the last

(3)

Many don't believe they existed
to begin with, no paper
trail or monuments or remains,
human or otherwise, no
manifestos or product lines

they lived imaginatively
in the space of negation
before calling themselves
Scriveners then calling

themselves nothing at all
their action of inaction
speaking for themselves

as they turned their backs
on us, on all of this, and said

I would prefer not to

(4)

*No problem is solved within
the mindset that created it*
their creed read around the

spiraling earthworks, remediated
heartbeds, enclaves open to all

but enclaves nonetheless. Their
energies, physic and erotic,
rerouted through meditation,
recooperative economics,

pills and soft-tech, liquid
states of desire *I want*
I want I want alchemized

into *earthconnection* until
they accepted the Earth

had become uninhabitable

(5)

After millennia of searching
they found it: The Fountain
of Youth, *Lifespring,* a greened
and lily-laden bank vibrating
within all that gray. They found

the water not only made them

young again but also rejuvenated
the Earth but only when tendered
in cupped human hands and

released in rivulets between
their fingers. They formed veins
and arteries, branching chains

passing water hand over hand
as far as their faulty vessels allowed

until The Fountain too dried up

(6)

The band got back together
untombed from junkyards
across the former continent
of North America their metal
frames rusty under molted faux

fur they polished each other's
chrome stitched themselves
back together with upholstery
from abandoned loveseats

Chuck E. Cheese, Helen Henry,
Jasper T. Jowls, Mr. Munch,
Pasqually E. Pieplate activated

other animatron immune to the
virus that killed all post-2k tech

and roved and ravaged and sang

Shawnda Wilson

Coverless Manhole

Back on the sofa
A.H.'s living room
left arm crooked   behind head
head lolled, neck tilted to point of looking broken

In his lap
antique plastic bag of pills and powders
good for nosebleeds and rolled up dollar bills

more bags beside and at his feet
a pillow pokes out, twenty maybe? bottles of supplements
and things like the laptop I gave up

things he may need   he thinks he made need all of these things
steel toed boots, brass knuckles, baseball bat, crowbar
the wool blanket his grandfather gave him last time

carries them couch to couch
fills his car with things he may need

We play tug-o-war

my fingers rope-burned
knees skinned and mud in my hair

but again I say yes
when he asks me to play

again
again
again

I am never the right answer

she put me out Ma
I was throwing up Ma
please leave she said Ma
I have nowhere to go
please Ma

In the car now and
I am always crying
he keeps napkins in the glove compartment
only it is full of handgun

'What is this?' I ask a stupid question
'Don't wanna talk about it' is his right answer

I grew this in my body

this animal rescue volunteer - cleaning shit, so much shit
this harm reduction outreach worker - the lives saved, so many lives
this beat up a roommate
this stealing-selling survivor
this hip hop star   bright star

Child,
what
in the world can I give you - that you would take
but not another pill
not another rail
or bloody nose
the staph infections

Where are your anonymous friends?
The ones who gave you god like a hanky

He's on the couch at A.H.'s house
someone slams a door
his head shoots up

"What?"

those plastic bags piled around him

like pylons circling a coverless manhole.

Atma Frans

On the Helpless Grass

The apple tree is down, branches
weeping amid the shattered fruit

—assaulted by a bear
while she just stood there, trunk curved,

drinking in the moon
 —like me that other night.

His heavy body. Foliage
a poor defence.

Teeth pierced the fruit
again and again and again.

The beast oblivious
to the snapping of heartwood

the scattering of my dying bits
—crazed

by the rippling of muscles,
his power

over my branches
spread on the helpless grass.

I kneel
beside her

with sticks and twine
and knowing hands

I lift her.

Daniel Damiano

You Can't Ask Friends to Help You Move Anymore

There used to always be at least two you could call upon
who were willing to move a cherry wood armoire
down a slender stairwell
of a 3-floor walk-up
on a Sunday
before the leaves changed;
that was when sciatica
wasn't a part of the vocabulary,
before bad knees would become
a valid excuse.
Now when that fateful day comes
to gather your decade or so of amassed life
in boxes
and sheets
and newspapers,
there isn't even a thought,
a possibility that you and your old friends
of 15, 20, 30 years
can do this,
with cold beer and pizza
the sole reward.

Now there's aching backs,

arthritic limbs,

throbbing appendages

that answer your proposal

before you can even fruitlessly ask,

leaving you now to pay strangers

who you have no history with,

who you watch struggle to navigate

your wooden bookcases

around an absurdly svelte hallway turn,

and yet,

        despite their every grunt and curse at the gods of city

architecture,

you envy the movers' elasticity,

          and how they are all at least 20 years

       from the maladies

          that have befallen

             your old friends.

To an Absent Confessor

I'll admit I read library books in the bathroom
and think negative thoughts as I chant "om" with *love* and *peace*
stones
clasped in each hand,
and that I think of money far too much
because of having far too little,
and I'll admit I question the legitimacy of movements –
not the bowel kind, but societal –
and how they tend to become waves of jerking knees
as opposed to a justifiable kneeing of jerks,
and I'll admit that rainy days make me sad and give me migraines
and that the sun tells me to smile, and I instinctively oblige,
and I'll admit I envy others luck,
so often blind or near-sighted,
and that I don't like getting older but don't wish that I were younger,
and I'll admit I eat too much cheese and drink too much coffee
and bloat between 3 and 4pm
and wonder what it takes to get toned abs when I have
hypothyroidism

and I'll admit I started jogging this morning
and felt God's hand gently caressing my palpitating heart
as my throat burned
and my wheezing didn't subside until lunch,

and I'll admit that I can't sleep sometimes,
and often when I do
I receive visitations from the dead,
and then I think of how life is so formless,
so intangible,
so mystical
and strange,
and then I wake up
...and I'll admit,...

        I'm glad that I did.

Charlie Dickinson

placebo

i carve out my hippocampus and amygdala

present them on the silver platter of treacherous images and

persistent memory

prized pigs

this way, no one can accuse me of false pretenses

let it be known—

i like the way the words climb through your soul and out your throat

back-breaking effort

yet your eyes play tricks on me

big and dark

cloudless recesses, bouncing off my own

shallow pools

i reflect my heart in my eyes

you know i always have

but reflections show backwards

i like to think yours are honest

i like to think yours say what i mean

but really, i think there's a hidden emptiness inside

(a river that'll never find home)

i stop, drop, and roll back and forth

on the knowledge that men lie
and on the knowledge that they are empty, devoid
of thought
it is narcissistic and naïve
to believe everyone is like me
equally so to feel that i am unique
but most of all, to dare to entertain, to think
that i, assigned female at birth, know best
whichever side i end up rolling to stop on

so let me set the record straight
i cut out my heart
messy and torn, like an attempt at paper chains
i carve out my hippocampus and amygdala
to make it clear what i truly remember and truly feel
let it be known, once and for all,
with nothing left but my frontal lobe
set against a self-portrait of death, i realize
my wings are bent and i've been circling this cage

struck iceberg

nails skim the edge of a pond—
a trail of ripples follows ominously
soundless on a chalkboard

my fingers reach in—
the kiss of cold waves
the shallow end of a lake, on a sunny summer day

imagining the way my knuckles dance—
sing "twinkle, twinkle, little star" to the fishes
fishes who have X-ray vision, who know my ultraviolet mind

the river swallows my palm whole—
greedy now, too late to go back for seconds
blue veins burst in synchrony

lips press glassy water, fall through—
swish the offending waves around behind my teeth
i wish water slid down my throat like milk

one last look to the horizon—
a grey balloon rises in the east
i bite the tip of my thumb methodically

do you remember how it is to be eight years old—

how it is to be eighteen

when the roar tears the words right out of your mouth

duck my nose beneath the surface—

eyes peeled wide, stinging with clarity

the hum fills my head again

the TV static of unconsciously held breaths, instinctually boxed

ears—

ocean threading my bones

the cold comfort of sinking below bloody blue foam

Annette Gagliardi

Addiction

Her Pall Malls lay on
the night stand, next to

the oxygen cord;
its tether snaking

to the five-liter tank
in the other room.

She gasps as she
waits

for me to turn
the machine on

and fill her line
with air.

As she adjusts
the nasal cannula,

her panic subsides.
A single tear

slides into the
crease between

her mouth and nose.
She slowly smiles

and reaches for
the Pall Malls,

caresses the edges
of the box, then

places them on
her nightstand again.

Bewildered

Public erasure tends
                    to fragment
and cancel old myths held too
close to   be revealed.
Our singular memories   cut
with the cheeky irreverence
          of the woodcutter's ax,
remind us that we can never go home again.

Rewind the stories told by the brothers,
Grimm and Hans Christian Anderson.
          Remember what the swans
sang by night, their light lit
by the little matchgirl warming
the dark. Dancing toes
          and boots marching
steadfastly—completing legend's mystique.

Chimera

Mothers and their babies carry
a piece of each other:
the scent, the feel, the sight
of their beloved.

They carry dreams of heaven,
figments of nirvana
hidden within and brought along
for the rest of their life,

its substance stuck inside each
breath, each heartbeat—symbiotic,
mutual admiration. Mothers
can also transform into ancient fire-breathers—

infants into goats that bleat and bunt, lions
that roar in the night—their DNA
sequences warped and misshapen,
writhing like a serpent's tail.

Is it delusion or dream—a mirage
of loveliness or genetic wish fulfillment,
that keeps them nurturing each other, despite
the impossibility of their task?

Humility

It's not death
        that devastates, especially
for those who believe in an afterlife.

It is the demeaning decay of
        the body that once was
vibrant and capable, that we fear.

Embarrassing reduction of abilities,
debasing *'procedures'* that examine
        and evaluate the rate of our decline.

We are introduced to *better life through medication;*
        maintenance by apparatus that reminds us
we are closer to the exit than ever before.

Yet we hang on while new exercises and habits
get us *up and going,*
        using paraphernalia that assists in our humiliation.

Degraded and diminished, we are kept alive
with reduced capacity and dwindling viability.

The collapse of what was, no longer supports our newly

undignified selves—mortification being our new garment.

Masquerade

The trees flamed at the retreating
sun, mirrored in its light.
Hemlock and Bloodroot
smote the shafts
of dusk and unfurled their scent
into the bloom of evening.

Crickets bow a twilight tune;
tensions drain off the day—
getting us ready for shadow
and moonglow.

Only a slivered smudge of
moon tonight—the darkness
overtakes everything. Soft
sounds dot the silence, mimic
movement of creatures scurrying to keep
up appearances that '*All is well*'

even though we all know that Night
Things will swallow what
they will—it shall be us or someone
quite close. I move deeper
into the underbrush and stop

breathing until morning.

S.I. Hassan

I'm So White

My bank manager knows my name. I'm so white,
she calls me Sandy. She gave me free tickets to the
rugby sevens tournament in Langford. My father said,
Your real name is Zandra
El-din Elnigar Abdelbar Ibrahim Hassan but
I'm so white, that sounds like 9/11.

With my white skin, he'd joke,
I must have come from the milkman.
Ya Ugly Hosam! his Arab pals exploded,
That's a good thing! Their loud laughter
embarrassed me in front of my
white friends who'd laugh whenever I said
Uncle Fahmy's[1] name. I'm so white that
I laughed along with them.

I'm as white as a spelling mistake blotted
out by liquid paper. As white as my speech
therapist scrubbing my tongue clean

---

[1]

     Pronounced fuchme

of impurity. As white as colours
fading,

merging,

melting away

into the hot pot of "Canada" in the 1970's.

I'm so white, but in the right light,
I look a little exotic. I stomp
to the rhythm, my hips swell
to the beat, I have howled
with grief and talk
with my hands, but I'm so white,
I didn't burden my white children
with any of my scary names.

No one asks me where I'm from,
no one tells me to go home,
no one would celebrate my return.

I didn't learn my father's tongue. *For what?*
he'd ask, *You? In a Muslim country?*
Imagine!
With that big mouth?

But now, he's gone.
Even my mom has forgotten

where I'm from.
We buried my brown and
I'm as white
as Assimilation's wet dream.

session one: our therapist asks me, why?

i ring the bell, you fold
yourself up, make yourself
invisible, show up late
with kindness and amnesia
you are trying
to sell me
your wholesome ideals
i am trying
to be
murky and real
i stopped buying
you stopped prying
long ago.

let's not
quarrel. let's be
grateful and honorable. we
saw this coming, played
hide and seek longer
than intended, counted to ten
a million times over.
even our kids are adults,
gosh darnit, liberated
from childish games

like avoidance and
disappointment.

listen, say the poets,
we're just miracles of circumstance,
in gravity's grip,
celestial donations,
super nova's transitory drips,
held under a spell of stability.

we should be dancing.

maybe i sound impractical now
like i trust myself – a little
out of control
like i want to be found – a little
wild child meets
old woman who pulls
we in close, sucks
we into the void, sings
songs of death, jumping
off cliffs, landing in nets

maybe the kids will think we're brave
maybe we can show them something different

DS Maolalai

Charming

walking on the southside
just over the river. north
of the liberties, christchurch
and toward inchicore.
a man in a corner
in an alley with a sickle
of ass looking up
from his belt-line – a woman
puts a needle in his ass. life
is all pigeons and bits of torn
paper on brickwork held
slick by old rainfall – I'm walking
with a shopping bag home. stopping
for a beer on the corner right next
to the mechanic who works
on my car when my car's out of service.
the evening is sinking like milk
into tea. tendrils of light in the darkness
come in around corners. I drink deep –
the windows all point at the road.
some americans talk about

how charming it is – dilapidation.

.

Something is happening

god damn. the flame
of this bus stop.
this clench of events
which are happening
now. a man scratches. a woman
moves pressure from one leg
to the other. someone's forgetting
the cost of their trip – checking
their pockets for change. people talk
about scenes in a narrative
as if catharsis must leak
from a fist between fingers. but
something is happening
always – the world
is a ball moving slowly
through space. that's interesting –
people on it are waiting
for transport – even if someone
doesn't fuck someone else. life
is a wild crawling animal, hard tooth
and red tongue, a sloppy of raw steak
and dripping. blood moves – things fly – there's
above us a pigeon. god damn it,
the flame of this bus stop. I'm going

somewhere. everyone

is going

somewhere.

Aram Martirosyan

Car am Car

I am a decent guy, working hard at the office to punch the clock with
furious triumph,
and go home.
I drive my decent car to my decent house
to my decent family
I have a car
I worked for the car
I drive the car
I am the car

I am Car

Car am Car

Car think that Car am "I",

but Car killed "I"

in a head-on collision

Car am a mass-produced product of silky-smooth advertisements
about rugged independence, uncharted lands, and horsepower
Car am made of the blood and bones of a sickly Mother Earth
Car am just part of the same traffic as everyone else,
blanketed by our collective smog of delusion and apathy
Car honk the horn, but no one listens
Car am swerving, drifting, driving
to wretched appointments, obligations, respites

Car dream of driving on the PCH toward a horizon, to nowhere, forever
Car am filled with dust, sentimental garbage, emergency supplies, and
items may one day come in handy—even though they haven't so far
Car hang up air fresheners to mask the unfortunate stench of the interior
Car shuffle through the radio to balance having fun and staying informed
Car am a bastion of culture
Car am a shell of ego without a sense of self
Car have no direction(s) and am asking for them all the time
Car am fine on the ground because Car was never meant to be a plane
Car will be shredded at the junkyard and evaluated in parts, pieces, and
pounds
Car am easy to mold and replace
Car am dead, and Car have killed him
Car am dead, but my driver gives me
the illusion that Car am alive,
and Car am fine with that

Callie Miller

Knocked Over

The soil spilt from the pot wants to go back in.
Like a breeze or clawing vines
Could help collect the damp mess.
It's been eleven minutes since it tipped
And the terra cotta becomes dual toned
Mildew and muddy
Rather than seeping its water into the carpet.

I lie on the floor and imagine worms
Slinking back into the ground
Imagine the snag of torn leaves
Plucked leaves
Once buried, upturned.
Now the question to be upright.

There is a vibration in my cheek
Pressed into the cocoa-dusted floor—
Sod, topsoil, too bitter for me.
A plate shift
A sandy fragment
And the pot will crack.
The stems look me in the eyes
Comfortably.

It's like rolling off the bed

Like tilted shelves and shattered picture frames

The 7am garbage truck

And a funeral.

Summer Ending

Desperately, we cling to the warm weather,
The sun run, light flood, big branches of summer.
Birds still prepare for flight.
Those of us waiting for a chill,
A sign from our brittle and shaking bones,
Have grown impatient.
Ignore the air getting lighter,
Ignore splitting lips and cracking knuckles.

I have now woken up exactly twice
Feeling the expectant cold of September.
There is a tumble of sheets that lie dormant on my bed
With knots and knots and fighting sleep.
Waking in a sweat is uncomfortable
       While the crisp of frost holds my flowers
       On the porch below me.

Something doesn't feel right
In the way my legs cross each other
The way that gourds don't mean autumn anymore.
Show me an escape to two years ago
When we yelled in the cornfield. It rained on our gaping mouths
And being lost in something of a child's game
       wasn't so bad.

Now the dried up, nude cornstalks
Tell me that running will get me no further.
Tell me I have reached the center of the maze and
Not even the dirt caked under my heels can feed me.

My sweat drenched sheets of corn-dreams will cold wash
And tumble dry. Right after I pulley my freight trained body from the
window.

Today the light of dewy morning becomes less dewy
And dims to 57 degrees. But I get out of bed
To another 90-degree day,
Sweat perched on my lip,
And my knees swollen like waterlogged bricks.
They keep me down and force me to trudge
Through nothing but the last days of summer.

Contributors

Drew Kiser is a PhD candidate in English at the University of California, Berkeley. Drew Kiser's works of fiction and criticism have appeared in *Full Stop*, *Polychrome Ink*, *MAKE magazine*, and *Maudlin House*. He can be reached on Twitter @drewkiser666.

DW Ardern is a fiction writer, humorist, and screenwriter living in Brooklyn, NY with a mischievous rabbit named Hazel and too many books. His stories have appeared (or are forthcoming) in *The Fourth River, Quagmire Literary Magazine, Stanchion, Vestal Review, Best Microfiction 2023 anthology, Fictive Dream, Jabberwock Review, Oyster River Pages*, and *The Offbeat* among others. He is the founding editor of *EXCERPT*, a lit art magazine for emerging fiction, film, music, and performance. He can be found on the interwebs at @mythosvsrobot (Twitter) and @mythosvstherobot (Instagram).

Kirk Vanderbeek (he/him) is a writer of fiction, poems, screenplays, comics. His work has been purchased by *Falling Star Magazine, Cosmic Horror Monthly, Ahoy Comics* and various alt weeklies. He lives in Southern California with his wife and son. You can typically find Kirk hunched over his laptop in any number of nooks or crannies into which he's managed to squeeze himself, pecking away at his current project. Disturb him if you must, he's awfully friendly.

Nikki Ummel is a queer writer, editor, and educator at the University of New Orleans. Nikki has been published or is forthcoming in *Painted Bride Quarterly*, *The Adroit*, *Hobart*, *The Georgia Review*, and more. In 2021, she was nominated for a Pushcart Prize in Poetry and awarded an Academy of American Poets Award. She is currently the Associate Poetry Editor for *Bayou Magazine*. You can find her on the web at www.nikkiummel.com.

Egill Atlason has a bachelor's degree in English from the University of Iceland, where he attended a creative writing workshop. His work has been published in the Icelandic magazine *Skandali*, and he's self-published a collection of parodies titled: *Fantabulous Fan Fiction*.

Chandler Dugal is a young and dedicated emerging writer. He lives a life of contradictions, but embraces them forthrightly. Chandler is a graduate student at Penn State University, and plans to attend law-school after obtaining his master's in public administration. Unfortunately, he is a currently incarcerated individual, but the experience has been a life changing and perspective altering one; arming him with aspirations for the future and a firm resolve to live a life of purpose and beneficence. Maine is his home, and his love of history is second only to his love of family.

Aaron Salzman is a writer and graduate student at the University of Alaska Fairbanks, where he is working on a combined MFA/MA degree. He's spent over one hundred days in the woods and wilderness on trips across North America; by car, canoe, train, and boot. His work is forthcoming in *The*

Artful Dodge. He lives in Fairbanks, where he enjoys salmon fishing and extra sunlight.

Suzanne Johnston is a writer and marketing professional from Calgary, Alberta. She writes short and novel-length fiction for adults, drawing inspiration from her prairie roots. Her work has appeared in publications such as *The Saturday Evening Post*, *Broken Pencil*, *Montreal Writes*, and *Agnes and True*.

Owen Schalk is a student in the MFA in Writing program at the University of Saskatchewan. He is also a columnist at *Canadian Dimension magazine* and a frequent contributor to other publications, such as *Alborada*, *Monthly Review*, and *Liberated Texts*. Additionally, his fiction has been published by a variety of print and digital publications, including *Fairlight Books*, *Sobotka Literary Magazine*, and *antilang*.

Bree Taylor is a writer and poet living on Treaty Six Territory in Canada. She is currently pursuing her B.A. at the University of Alberta, where she has won the L. June Kelly Prize in Introductory Poetry. Her fiction has appeared in "Liminal Space: A Debut Student Anthology," and her poetry has appeared in *3 Moon Magazine*, *C&P Quarterly*, *Funicular*, the *Celestial/Bodies anthology*, and in a forthcoming chapbook called "How To Get A Thigh Gap" that she co-authored with Nisha Patel. She was a finalist for the Dell Award for Undergraduate Excellence in Science Fiction and Fantasy Writing in 2022. You can find her on Twitter at @BreeTaylor0.

POETRY

Tyler French (he/him/his) is a queer writer and organizer living in Waterville, ME. His first full-length book of poetry,

He Told Me was published by *Capturing Fire Press* in 2019. He has writing in *Assaracus, Beech Street Review, Bending Genres Journal, Impossible Archetype,* and *The Quarry,* Split This Rock's Social Justice Poetry Database. He is a co-creator and baker for Queer Cookies, a poetry series, bake sale, and poetry/cookbook celebrating LGBTQ+ poets.

Shawnda Wilson is a visual artist, poet, writer of fiction and creative dreamer. She has published numerous chapbooks with titles such as "Muses on a Tight Rope" and "Fear is Free." Her work has been featured in *Portal Mag, Island Writer, Four Minutes to Midnight* among others. She has won awards such as the Mary Garland Coleman award for lyric poetry and the Bill Juby award for excellence. Long listed for the Bridge Prize summer 2022, Shortlisted for This Side of West competition fall 2022, Second Prize winner of Quagmire Magazines first poetry contest among others. She lives to read, create, teach and share.

Atma Frans searches for the voice beneath her personas: woman, architect, mother, teacher, queer, poet. Her work has been a finalist for contests and is published internationally including in *The New Quarterly, Arc Poetry Magazine, CV2, Understorey Magazine, The Dalhousie Review, Prairie Fire Magazine, Chiron Review, Obsessed with Pipework, Lighthouse Literary Journal.* She lives on the traditional territory of the Sḵwx̱wú7mesh people (Gibsons, B.C.) in Canada. For further info see: www.spacestobe.org

Daniel Damiano is an Award-Winning Playwright, Actor, Novelist and Poet based in Brooklyn, NY. His poems have appeared in *Curlew Quarterly, Crooked Teeth Literary Magazine, Cloudbank, Newtown Literary Journal,* New Voices Anthology 2016 and HotMetal Press. He was a 2012 nominee for the Pushcart Poetry Prize. In 2021, his debut poetry book, "104 Days Of The Pandemic," was published by fandango 4 Art House. He has also published two acclaimed novels, "The Woman in the Sun Hat" (2021, Seattle Book Review Recommendation) and, in December 2022, "Graphic Nature," also through fandango 4 Art House, along with his first collection of full-length plays, "Plays By Daniel Damiano - Volume 1." His acclaimed play "Day Of The Dog" was published in 2018 by Broadway Play Publishing.

Charlie Dickinson has been committed to writing since he was eight, with a passion for poetry from the age of fourteen. This love of writing began with reading the Little House books by Laura Ingalls Wilder.. Since then he's continued to write in multiple forms, taking inspiration from punk music, anthropology, and art history. Affectionately known as a "book freak, Charlie also loves travelling, attending writing workshops, learning about people, and seeking out new experiences. Charlie dreams to be a part of something worthwhile, and to be happy.

Annette Gagliardi has been writing poetry since the early 1980's, is active in her area chapter and state poetry association and still finds time to bake, garden, quilt and volunteer at church and nearby schools. She also writes books and has two children's books published. Her most recent work is titled: "A Short Supply of Viability" and is a full-length poetry collection that discusses the role of caregiving. Annette's work can be found on Amazon as well as her author website (https://annette-gagliardi.com/)

S.I. Hassan is a writer living on Legungwen territory writing about the complexities of family, culture and climate change. Hassan is about to embark on their MFA journey at the University of Victoria. Hassan was recently shortlisted for the *Malahat Review* Constance Rooke CNF prize and that piece will be published by them this spring.

DS Maolalai has received eleven nominations for Best of the Net and eight for the Pushcart Prize. His poetry has been released in three collections; "Love is Breaking Plates in the Garden" (Encircle Press, 2016), "Sad Havoc Among the Birds" (Turas Press, 2019) and "Noble Rot" (Turas Press, 2022).

Aram Martirosyan is a writer of variety and wit. Two of his poems are in literary magazines from his alma mater, Hampshire College. He's an experienced reader, having done open-mic nights in Los Angeles, Amherst, MA, and New York, including venues like The Last Bookstore, Skylight Books, Nuyorican Poets Cafe, and the Pilipino Workers Center. Aside from the poetry, Aram has responses published in Wall Street Journal's "Future View" series. One discusses the appeal of Bernie Sanders to young voters and the other discusses what young people expect from their employers. Lastly, Aram appeared on the podcast "I Care, Do You?" discussing narratives of genocide in foreign policy.

Callie Miller is a poet, freelance writer, and book editor from Denver, Colorado where she studied creative writing at the University of Denver. Callie has written poetry for 12 years and is currently working on her second manuscript. Callie's work has been published in *Foothills*, *Cicada Creative*, and *Caveat Lector*.

Manufactured by Amazon.ca
Bolton, ON

34041572R00085